FROM THE MOUTH OF THE WHALE

ALSO BY SJÓN

The Blue Fox

From the Mouth of the Whale

Sjón

Translated from the Icelandic
by Victoria Cribb

TELEGRAM

ISBN: 978-1-84659-083-2

First published as *Rökkurbýsnir* by Bjartur, Reykjavík, in 2008

This English edition published in 2011 by Telegram

A full CIP record for this book is available from the British Library.

A full CIP record for this book is available from the Library of Congress.

Printed and bound by CPI Cox & Wyman, Reading, RG1 8EX

TELEGRAM
26 Westbourne Grove, London W2 5RH
www.telegrambooks.com

This book has been published with financial support from Bókmenntasjóður / The Icelandic Literature Fund

'Soon it seemed to him that the stars had become men,
the men stars, the stones beasts,
the clouds plants ...'

Novalis, *The Novices of Sais*

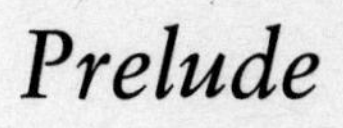
Prelude

I was on my way home from the hunt. In my right hand I held my net, in my left a lantern, and in the pack slung over my back was my prey, a wild boar with tusks of steel; a colossal beast that had run amok in the lands of the north, wreaking havoc until the alarm was raised and I was charged with hunting it down. It was not the first of the North Wind's monstrous brood that I had laid low – the wolf that wept tears of milk, the one-footed water hare, the bull elk with the golden pizzle and the queen of the shag-haired trout had all made acquaintance with my net – but this huge-tusked boar was without doubt the most savage brute the north had ever snorted from its icy nostril.

Instead of leaving the carcass on the bloody field as the laws decreed, I brought it with me, intending to cast it at my brothers' feet. Then the Father would see which of his sons laboured hardest to keep our world in check: those who never stirred from the all-encompassing paternal abode where they occupied themselves with administrative business (such was the euphemism for courtly life), or I who flew far and wide, dispatching monsters.

The void crunched under my heels as I strode homeward. Ahead the evening meal awaited me in the glorious, scintillating palace with all its towers and spires streaming into space like the babbling of a newborn sun. I meant to rise to my feet between the main and dessert courses, walk over to my brothers and whip the steel-tusker from my pack. But I had not gone far before I perceived that all was not well in Seventh Heaven. There was no watch at the gate, no call of 'Ho, who goes there?' from the ramparts, no sound of merrymaking from the banqueting hall, no lovers enjoying a secret tryst in the gateway. Instead, my trained hunter's ears caught the rustle of nervous wings and the anguished moans that stick fast in the throat. I threw down my lantern, net and pack. Next moment I was in the courtyard; an instant later I was running up the steps to the throne room where I flung open the doors.

Conditions in the chamber were sickening; many of the angels were laughing with fear, others were weeping with hollow laughter, still others laughed and wept at once. The Ophanim had cast off their robes and knelt with brows pressed to the cold steps of the throne, letting fly with knotted scourges on their blazing shoulders. The youngest brothers were running around the chamber as aimlessly as babes, ceaselessly screeching their father's name. The most sensitive were slumped against pillars and benches, vomiting spasmodically, the ectoplasm gushing from their mouths to flow unchecked over the azure floors of Heaven. Underlying the hideous spectacle was the whispering sound that is formed when sheer despair filters out into the flight feathers, causing the soft plumes to tremble and the air to play over them with a shrill whistling like a blade of grass blown by a child; it was this sound that had breached the encircling walls of the palace and carried to me on my homeward road: the true alarm call of the angels.

'He is dead!'

The thought, lancing my mind, left my body momentarily stunned: the unthinkable had happened! I was on the verge of losing control of myself when I noticed the stench. An odour reached my nostrils, an odour never before smelt in my father's house and hitherto outlawed in Heaven. For the worlds He created, with all their creatures and plants, and His own world were prohibited from meeting; like light and darkness, as He Himself decreed. Yet the stench that now tainted the air in His palace was the stench of blood and urine, sweat and sperm, mucus and grease.

I looked at the Father, who was lounging at ease on His throne. From His manner you would have thought all was well in paradise; His ice-bright head was lowered a little as He examined something small in His palm. At His left hand stood my brother Michael, apparently the only one to be in control of his feelings. But I, who knew Michael better than anyone, saw that the smile playing over his lips was the familiar grimace that he used to assume when admitting himself defeated in our games. He inclined his head slowly towards me, without taking his eyes off whatever it was our Father was holding.

Yes, there you lay in His hand, with your knees tucked under your chin, breathing so fast and so feebly that you quivered like the pectoral fin of a minnow. Our Father rested His fingertip against your spine and tilted His hand carefully so that you uncurled and rolled over on to your back. I stepped forward to take a better look at you. You scratched your nose with your curled fist, sneezed, oh so sweetly, and fixed on me those egotistical eyes – mouth agape. And I saw that this mouth would never be satisfied, that its teeth would never stop grinding, that its tongue would never tire of being bathed in the life-blood of other living creatures. Then your lips moved. You tried to say your first word, and that word was: 'I'. But the Father interrupted you and addressed me in an affable but commanding tone:

'Lucifer, behold Man! You must bow down before him like your brothers ...'

I looked at you a second time and in that instant you released a stream of slimy, black faeces. Quick as lightning, you shoved your hand under your buttocks, fetched a fistful of whatever you found there, and raised it to your mouth.

As all the world knows, I did not bow my knee to this new pet of my father's, and for that I was cast out of Heaven along with all who wished to follow me. But my parting gift to you, Man, is this vision of yourself.

I

(Autumn Equinox, 1635)

A medium-sized fellow ... Beady brown eyes set close to his beak within pale surrounds ... The beak itself quite long, thick and powerful, with a slight downward curve at the end, dark in colour but lighter at the top ... No neck to speak of; a spry, stocky figure with short, tapering legs, a barrel chest and a big belly ... Head a dark grizzled brown, with a ruff extending from nape to mid-crown ... Clad in a grey-brown coat of narrow cut, with a faint purple sheen in the twilight; bright stockings, a speckled undershirt ... Importunate with his own kind, garrulous with others ... So might one describe the purple sandpiper and so men describe me ... I can think of many things worse than being likened to you, my feathered Jeremiah, for we have both crawled from the hand of the same craftsman, been carved with the same knife: you quickened to life on the fourth day, I on the sixth ... But what if the order had been reversed? If I had entered the stage with those who soar beneath the firmament while you had been appointed lord of the Earth? Would a bird then be sitting here on a rock, thoughtfully watching the insensate man scurrying along the water's edge, querulous with fear that when the sea recedes from the land it might never return? ... Man and bird, man with a bird's heart, bird with a man's brain, bird with a man's heart, man with a bird brain ... We are alike in most things ... And why should we not be? Lately I held your skua-bitten brother in my hand and probed his corpse with my fingers ... Under the breast feathers I felt first sternum, then ribs, then the soft parts that contain kidneys and bowels ... And as I examined the bird I ran my free hand over my living body ... This was during the Dog Days, when the hot weather paid a visit to Gullbjörn's Island, and my self-examination was made easier by the fact that I was wearing nothing but my birthday suit ... I was free to walk about so, for I was alone with no one there to see me but the Master-smith, who, after all, knows all his works better than they know themselves ... There was no mistaking the Creator's template, for my whole body was cast in the same mould as my feathered friend ... Yet, although our vessels are almost identical, our life journeys are like the hands of two scribes who have learnt from a single exemplar and are now copying the same story, one seated under the sheriff's roof at Ögur, the other at the bishopric of Hólar, both taking care to read the manuscript aright ... Yet to an informed reader the ascender appears foreshortened on the 'd' of the scribe who works under the tyrants' patronage, whereas it exhibits an elegantly curved forward slant from the hand of the scribe who is the guest of God's representative during his flight from those same villains ... You, bird, are the letter that was deftly penned during a quiet hour in the Lord's house, whereas I must endure having my image scored out or scraped off the vellum by those who envy and hate me: 'Jónas is a rogue, Jónas is a sly, disreputable fellow, Jónas is a braggart, Jónas is a liar, Jónas is a foolish dreamer ...' Yes, thus am I portrayed in the slanderous letters and oral reports that precede me wherever I go ... I say this because, according to the old Jerusalemites, the building blocks of the world and its inhabitants were formed of the alphabet at the back of God's tongue when He pronounced the world, as if it were a tale so tremendous that no one but He Himself would live to hear it all; and wretched man is grateful for every hour that he is permitted the grace of hearing those scraps of the tale that concern him ... Little creatures like us two, Jónas and the sandpiper, are scarcely more than a word of the genus of the smallest words, formed from a single syllable: 'oh', 'ah', 'ee', 'ow' ... Words comprehensible to all, for so Adam's kin, 'the tormented ones', cry their name when sorrow comes upon them or one of them breaks a toe ... Now why did I think of the letter 'd' and not of some other? What does 'd' signify in Abraham Salómonsson's alphabetical tree? On what branch did that letter flower? Is it Daleth? Did a bird sit there chirping at the morning sun? Did a man hang upside down from a rope slung over the branch? Here I am blind, bereft of books ... You trip along at the foot of the glaciers, on the remotest shores, poking your kelp-brown beak into the grey sand, grateful for the strip of land allotted to you by the Lord ... Heaven besides, there is nothing more sought-after, and it is the most ardent prayer of well-nigh every human Icelander that exactly thus might they arrange their lives; here you are born, here you seek your sustenance and here you will die ... You are a delight to the eyes during your lifetime, sandpiper, and wherever you may be summoned after death, even then you often prove a source of pleasure ... Our acquaintance began half a century ago and five years more when a flight feather loosened from your decaying skin blew across the foreshore, in over the marshes, out over the farming district and high up the hillside to settle at the feet of my grandfather, Hákon Thormódsson, son of Thormódur, son of Salómon the boat-builder ... He had gone berry-picking with the boy Jónas and, despairing of preventing the child from stuffing the fruit in his mouth, had begun to sing me edifying verses, as was his custom when we were alone together ... That day it was Eysteinn's blessed 'Lily', and he had just reached the part where I always started to giggle, the description of Lucifer's visit to the suffering king on the holy tree ... I was six years old and well aware that my laughter was both foolish and sinful ... But from the moment he recited the first words of the praise poem I would dread his pronouncing 'peep at the cross, the devil did then', and the fear of losing control of myself tightened still further Folly's grip on my mind ... Naturally, the blame lay not with the glorious story of mankind's redemption nor with the poet's delightful verses, but with the mask that Grandfather assumed when he intoned the word 'peep' ... He would lean back with his weight on his left leg so his right shoulder lifted and the other one sank, simultaneously shooting up his eyebrows and pouting his lips to pronounce the word 'peep';

it was quite inadvertent, he was blithely unaware of the effect ... And I would dissolve into laughter ... Nothing seemed more absurd to me than the idea that the countenance of the hellish serpent Satan should have appeared as comical and mild to the Son of Man as my grandfather Hákon's expression did at that moment to me ... I hung my head and clamped both hands over my mouth but gouts of laughter spurted out between my fingers, quick as a horde of croaking demons escaping from a bag ... Grandfather stopped abruptly and subjected the child to grave scrutiny ... But in that instant the sandpiper's feather settled by the toe of his shoe ... He said:

'I think you're going to have a good memory, Jónas ...'

Grandfather squatted on his heels, levelling out the difference between us and, reaching for the feather, held it for a moment between his fingers before poking it into the hair above my right ear:

'And now we must teach you to read ...'

I used this purple-grey feather of yours as a pointer all the time it took him to teach me to read ... And this happy meeting between child's hand and quill also served to define the difference between boy and bird ... For although the tip of the quill touched the parchment as I stumbled from word to word, none of the wisdom found its way into you, sandpiper, but engraved itself entirely on my childish mind ... Though until the moment when I bent to my books our understanding had begun and ended in the domain of the flesh; in how our two minds interpreted the wind and the rain ... Oh, that I had never learnt to read! There old Jónas began his long march of torment over the libertine earth, scorched by the twilight portents of the Reformation, by the burning of holy crucifixes and the destruction of old books, while the little sea mouse lives on in innocence and blessed ignorance ... I do not doubt, feathered earth apple, that God's mother will look kindly on you, whether the Blessed Orb splinters into a thousand suns in the Easter dew on the wing that hides your simple head or the moon whitens your snowy breast during the vigil on Christmas night: remember this in the wild joy of the high tide and the despair of the spring ebb ...

'Twit-tweet ...' comes my answer from the beach and the sandpiper flies off the rock ... It flaps its stubby wings rapidly, heading out to sea, then veers abruptly and returns to shore, and in the brief instant that my eye follows its flight I catch sight of the blue rim of the mainland ... Otherwise one cannot see it from my seat here on top of the Gold Mound ... No, I prefer not to point so much as my cold nose in that direction ... How the sight perturbs my mind! It is too painful to smell the mingled perfume and putrid stench that emanate from that quarter ... I was ordered to clear off to this rock and from here there is no going back ... It is my home now ... On the blue horizon nothing but torture and thumbscrews await me; cudgels and slander, poisonous powder and serpents split to the groin so that they appear to walk on two legs ...

SEA-SPECKLE: *the smallest species of bird, known as the sea-speckle, scarcely measures a third of a sandpiper in size. It is spotted white and black, and thus we speak of speckled earth when the snow lies patchily on the ground. Men have at times hauled up a kind of seaweed, four or five fathoms long without its root, from which a little bird has hatched, though whether this is the sea-speckle or some other species we cannot tell.*

Four summers ago the serpent brothers condemned me to exile, decreeing that anyone who offered me a helping hand would suffer the same punishment ... On that terrible day, the site of the court was shrouded in libertine twilight ... I noticed one man turn away when the sentence was read out; the blessed vice-principal Brynjólfur Sveinsson, a handsome, promising man who was only a guest there, though prepared in all humility to assume the office of the late venerable Bishop Oddur Einarsson, one-time disciple of Tycho Brahe and student of astronomy at his observatory in Hven ... But the men of the south did not wish to accept the learned Brynjólfur's offer of service in God's acre, any more than they would suffer poor Jónas to administer his little spiritual plasters to the earthly afflictions of his neighbours ... For a brief instant there was a gleam of sunlight through the darkness that loured over that assembly of wolves ... As Nightwolf Pétursson's hired thugs were driving me from the court with blows and ape-like howls, the younger brother of my old enemy, Sheriff Ari Magnússon of Ögur, saw his chance to trip me up at the gate, for the further amusement of the hyenas ... A fall was prepared for me, but even as I was flying headlong into the mud, I felt a soft hand stroke along the chain where the irons chafed worst, and I was able to leave the court with my head held high … Throwing a quick glance over my shoulder I spotted Brynjólfur's right hand vanishing into the sleeve of his cloak, for he it was who stood by the gatepost, but I could not fail to see that his wrist was guided by another hand, of milk-white maternal perfection: it was the Virgin Mary who led him to perform this act of mercy towards the miserable wretch for whom all succour was now banned by the law of the land … Blessed is he who is chosen as her instrument … That night all my wounds ceased their bleeding and filled the whole dungeon with the sweet scent of the lily … Jónas is the exile who cannot go anywhere … Twit-tweet … Whereas the sandpiper can fly away if his courage fails … But what might his piping 'twit-tweet' signify? Nothing, fortunately; he is only saying good day … A bird with such trivial news to impart surely harbours no bezoar in his skull … Twit-tweet … His low-lying brain-pan has nothing to offer the natural philosopher … No one would bother to ensnare him in order to char his little head since there is nothing of value concealed there: no healing stone or philosopher's stone, no stone of any kind to protect against disorders of the blood or mind ... No, there is no bezoar there ... Bezoar! But I was not going to think about bezoar today ... Bezoar! Bezoar! Bezoar! A volume containing scraps of wisdom from the works of Master Bombastus Paracelsus, translated from the German to Icelandic and inscribed with the name of the old schoolmaster at Skálholt, which arrived in Steingrímsfjord by crooked paths and was always hidden under my grandfather's bed when strangers came to visit; this was the book from which I learnt to read and the first I learnt by heart ... After which I read the old Saga of Bishop Gudmundur Arason ... In that order ... And things went as they did ... For that is how my trials began, and who could have guessed that I would end up on this bird-fouled rock, this dance floor of seals? ... But oh, what a joy it was to read! Once the letters had acquired their correct sounds and arranged themselves into words which I knew from my own speech and that of others; when the conjunction of the words begat all the explanations of the world and stories that together furnished my head from within, as if its bony vault were the walls of the gallery and libraries of the University of Copenhagen ... places I will never see ... For I am condemned to sit here alone, chattering to the foolish bird that most closely resembles me ... Yes, sandpiper, let us not deceive ourselves about the rung we occupy on the ladder of human society ... Although you can spread your wet wings and capture with them the far-travelled sunbeam, and I can hold up my thumb and forefinger till the moon is pinched between their tips like a pearl, neither of us will be able to hold on to our lucky catch ... Enough of that, enough about you and enough about me; there is another they wish me to address and he is as grim as you are tender ... I will not do it ... No one can be expected to escape alive from wrestling with ancient revenants of dreadful power ... I escaped from such an ordeal once before and doubt I could do so again ... I would have done better to have kept quiet, kept my damned trap shut, instead of going around spewing out everything that shot up to the surface of the bottomless well of information and useless ideas that book-reading had etched in the leaf-mould of my mind, all boiling and bubbling like a potion in a magic cauldron ... But no, of course I could not be quiet ... I was forever blathering of bezoar ... whose name alone is as intoxicating as the scent of the forbidden blossom on the Tree of Knowledge ... I was drunk on the very idea of such a stone that could not only heal all human ailments but also prove useful to alchemists wise in the ways of converting base metal to gold ... Wherever I went, wherever I broke my journey, I would ask after the carcass of a raven ... Had anyone chanced upon a dead raven in the last few days or weeks? Yes, that is how it began ... And should anyone remember having seen a dead raven, I would be off in a trice to examine it ... Then one could find the child Jónas crawling into holes or scrambling up crags to retrieve the rotting hide of *Corvus islandicus* ... For it was and still is my belief that the bezoar must be much more potent in the Icelandic raven than in its namesake elsewhere, on account of its affinity with that King of Fools, Odin, and his heathen tribe here in the north of the world ... At any rate, I was nine years old when I began my quest for the cranial stone, which has now lasted fifty-three winters with no sign of success ...

'Look, here comes Hákon with his grandson; I don't suppose he'll be able to keep the lad quiet for long before the little fool starts harping on about where he can find some damned dead crow ...'

Even when I stood silently at my grandfather's side while he talked to the old men about the kinds of things old men talk about, I could not fail to notice the glances, the pauses, the questions in which they hoped to trap me ... I used to maintain a stony silence until in the end I would tug Grandfather Hákon's coat sleeve and ask:

'Might I go and take a look in the kitchen, Grandpapa?'

Here was company more fitting for a youngster who had learnt to read from the writings of Dr Bombastus and acquired so great a knowledge of the abdomen that there was scarcely a female malady in existence that I did not have a nodding acquaintance with – I would always have a prescription up my sleeve for a poultice that would cure the affliction ... I used to take my learning and my requests for dead ravens into the heat and smoke with the womenfolk ... And from those kitchen visits I began to acquire something of a reputation as a physician ... 'Little Jónas the healer,' they would say, for that is what the womenfolk called me, 'give me some good news about this swelling I have ...' And the woman would grasp my hand and draw it under her clothes, laying it low down on her belly and dragging it back and forth over some lump in her flesh ... I would close my eyes and summon up the book of medical art until it lay there open before my nose, the verso folio inside my left eyelid and the recto inside my right ... Then I would turn the pages in my mind until I reached the part about that divinely created miniature likeness of man, woman, who must presumably obey the same laws of nature as the male, for he is a world in microcosm, made from the substance of the cosmos, and woman is made from his substance ... There on the page I would find accounts of the principal female ailments and compare these to the news my hand was reading from the corporeal page of the woman whom I was to cure ... Thus I read together book and woman until both merged into one and then all that was required was to read out the prescription for the medicine that accompanied the description of the disease ... Sometimes the medicines were to be boiled, sometimes kneaded, sometimes hot and sometimes cold ... But the examination always ended with my saying aloud:

'That bezoar would have come in handy now ...'

Once my collecting mania became known, it would invariably turn out that some old lady had chanced upon the rotting little brother of Odin's companions, Hugin and Munin, and taken the trouble to pull off its head and keep it in her pouch 'for Jónas' ... If a long time had passed since I last acquired a raven's head, I would be unable to rest from the moment I laid hands on it ... I would find some excuse to slip away and almost before the farm buildings were out of sight I would take out my tinderbox, gather a pile of kindling and burn the head ... I went about my quest in this way in obedience to my learned master Bombastus's instructions ... Once the head had been reduced to ashes the skull would be brittle and easy to crack open, and if luck was with me there should be a single specimen of bezoar inside, like an expectant chick in its shell ... But luck never was with me ... And I have lost count of the ravens' heads I have roasted and crushed in my lifetime ... Yes, those were my wages for the cures I used to perform in the kitchens of the Strandir folk, and it was a useful arrangement since Grandfather had made me swear a solemn oath that no raven would die by my hand ... Eventually, though, there came a time when my female patients no longer wanted my great fists fumbling under their skirts ... I was thirteen years old and examining a slightly peculiar old biddy whose appointed task was to bless the cows at the croft of Hólmskot when they were let out to graze in the morning ... She used to do this by calling on Saint Benedicta, and had arrived at such a good understanding with the celestial lady that the cows on that farm never failed in their yield ... Nevertheless, she thought it better to let me heal her than to place her trust entirely in the protection of the saints, for although they had been her helpmeets ever since childhood they had lately been abolished by law and banished from Icelandic homes, and now mainly took refuge with useless old folk, like this Hálotta Snæsdóttir, who was fated to awaken the puppy in me ... The healing session had proceeded as usual; one woman after another had received a gentle caress and diagnosis of her complaint, accompanied by good advice and hope of improvement, and now it was the turn of Hálotta who sat at the back of the room, contemplating some dried fish that was soaking there ... I had no sooner sat down beside her than she trapped my youthful hand in her blotchy old claw and shoved it under her skirts ... There were no surprises there, just the usual worn-out woman's belly, though the old lady was in fairly good nick ... She took charge and I sat in my physician's pose with head inclined and eyes closed, the book hovering before my mind's eye, but just as she was about to return my healing hand to me, my fingers came into contact with the upper limits of her *mons pubis* ... It was not as if it was the first time I had touched what I had heard the women themselves call half in jest their 'mouse', and the contours of the creature were fairly well known to me from diagrams in the books of medicine from Hólar ... But this time when my fingertips brushed so unexpectedly against old Hálotta's garden wall, I stiffened ... It was only an instant's response but enough for her to sense it; we were, after all, both in the same part of the old woman's anatomy ... As if to be certain of my miserable predicament, she made a pretence of pulling our hands down still further but this time I resisted in earnest ... Upon which she whipped my hand from under her skirt band and squealed:

'Ooh! He's not touching me there again – not unless he marries me!'

With that my youthful innocence was laughed away ... The time of the laying on of hands was over ... I had to find a new way to ingratiate myself with the old ladies who always had a raven's head ready to slip into the hand of a budding naturalist ...

—

MOONWORT: *Botrychium lunaria. One of the most potent of the herbs used in childbirth: to be laid on the cervix, the secret door or private parts, when a woman is about to deliver, and snatched away the instant the child is born to prevent the intestines or other parts from following. When administered to a patient it prevents lethargy and intensifies pleasure and recreation. Some believe it to have the virtue of opening locks. It is often found growing on old hayfield walls or ruins, but never in wetlands, and grows to half a finger in height. It proved of greatest virtue to me long ago when I was laid low with an intolerable whooping cough. I chewed it as small as I could, mixed with aqua vitae and thyme, no more than a tiny morsel at a time, but even that was enough. After that I did not catch a cough or cold for five years. It is more frequently used than other digestive herbs for internal cures but not for complaints of the flesh or skin. The moonwort bears sometimes twelve, sometimes thirteen leaves on one stalk, depending on the number of moons in the year when the earth is temperate; and seeds on the other, as many as the number of weeks that a mother carries her unborn child. Herbs should be used with caution.*

—

It was the custom at Grandfather Hákon's house for extracts to be copied from those among the books that found their way there which he judged to be most interesting and of most enduring value ... His method was to collect in one place all the lore and verses or tales true or invented touching on a particular subject that were found scattered among the various books he borrowed ... This amounted to something of an industry on Grandfather's part and his scriptorium consisted of a reader, a scribe and an ink-maker, the last-mentioned of whom concocted the ink as well as cutting the feathers for quills ... I was appointed special assistant to the ink-maker, 'Squinting' Helgi Sveinsson; a work-shy half-cousin of ours who had turned up on my grandparents' doorstep with a group of wandering beggars ... Even in that company he had managed to rub people up the wrong way and the beggars left him behind when it transpired that his family could be half traced to that of the householder ... My grandfather used to make all the paupers who boarded with him contribute something towards their keep ... Much of this was of limited value as the wretched people had small aptitude for anything, but every little counts in a large household; the cat may seem inclined to do nothing but lick her fur but we would soon be overrun by mice if we hanged her for her vanity ... On account of this half-cousin's feeble nature, the division of labour between us was quite contrary to what might be expected between a full-grown man and a boy ... I was the master and he the apprentice, but we took great care not to let it show who ruled the roost when it came to preparing the ink, and no one found out until I was moved up a rung in the scriptorium and seated in one of the scribes' chairs ... There I took a new, more ominous step on the path towards the evil destiny that finally forced me into exile in my own country ... Though what kind of exile is it, pray? I am condemned to forsake my homeland, no one may offer me a helping hand, wherever I am seen people are duty bound to arrest me and I may not linger for any space of time in any place without violating my sentence – which would give the villains an excuse to make my penalty even harsher, until ultimately I advance shrieking into the fires of hell ...

'Jónas Pálmason, by some called Jónas "the Learned", that is I, and may God bid you good day, Captain Sir ... I hear that you are sailing for England with a cargo of homespun cloth belonging to the Sheriff of Ögur – er, you wouldn't happen to have room for a homeless vagabond like me aboard this fine vessel of yours?'

Flat refusal ... No one is willing to transport Jónas from these shores ... Not even if he composes handsome verses about the rotting hulks that he longs with all his heart would take him away from Iceland ... For even so can a poet describe a ship that balances on nothing but a leaking, tarry hull:

The sail swells on the sea lion,
canvas cracks and sheets strain,
shrouds sing aloud to the wind's wild refrain.

Even foundering in the monster-filled deep in a tub like that would surely be better than languishing as a prisoner at home ... I long more than anything to go abroad ... I have so often visited foreign lands in my dreams, whether waking over illustrations in books or asleep in my bunk, only to find myself in that very city, usually on my way to a meeting with the wise men of the place ... With a long parcel in my hand; no mean gift and one that would look well in the chambers that house the finest treasures in the land ... Then a voice calls out in Icelandic: 'Look at Jónas!' And in that instant the outer appearance of the countrymen is transformed and they turn into grey maggots, crawling towards me, hissing foolishly: 'Look at Jónas!' ... And each of the slitherers has three human faces, one named Nightwolf, one named Ari, that is Eagle, and the third named Ormur, that is Serpent ... More bearable were the daydreams, glimpses through the windows of books that I once owned, although the desperate longing to go there in the flesh never resulted in anything more than mournful sighs over the wretched fate of being Jónas the Learned ... Perhaps my nature is bound to these icy shores ... Even if all the sheriffs and beggars in the land, all the judges and thieves, bishops and whores, squires and crofters clubbed together to apprehend the fellow and drive him out to sea, even then the ship would not travel far from shore with this sorry cargo before the crew would be forced to put out their boat and convey Jónas back to land ... For he would be assailed by an overwhelming attack of homesickness ... Ah, did you think I had forgotten you, sandpiper, or how my nature seems bound to yours, you Jónas of the bird world? No, hardly have you set your course out to sea than you turn back ... You did so a little while ago and now I see you repeating the game ... And then I remember that I have been sitting here far too long ... In England you are known as sandpiper. What should I be called there, I wonder? Jonah Palmson the Learned? I would like to fly there ... England has been described to me as the land where the Virgin Queen reigned with such modesty that her subjects thought they had acquired a new mother after gentle Mary had been taken from them ... A well-travelled man who had visited London told me that he had met an old man there, Benjamin Jonson the actor, a quarter Icelandic and as well-informed about life in the palaces as on the streets of the capital ... He drew a fair picture of the queen, saying that the noble Elizabeth lived like a holy maid on her throne, for her flesh was never sullied by any man; her insides were innocent of all male outpourings ... And no lord dared so much as raise a finger against her for fear of drawing down upon himself the ire of the people ... For although her delicate virginal breasts were quite unlike the divine bosom of the Holy Mother, and devoid of the white balsam that heals the deepest wounds, yet such sisterly mildness shone from her breast that even her most inveterate enemies would shed tears and fall to their knees with clasped hands ... They thanked her even as their heads were lopped from their bodies ... But she was harsh to papists – and she will not be forgiven for that – although the Bishops' Church in her English realm is not shrouded in the same fetid, satanic darkness as ours here in Iceland, nevertheless it was just as ugly a deed to deprive the people of their saints ... For to whom is a person to turn when the powerful break the law in their dealings with the innocent, caring neither for their honour nor for the final reckoning on Doomsday? At times like that it was a comfort to be able to turn to the blessed Virgin Mary, and John the Apostle, and Saint Barbara, or to Luke who will do anything for a painter, or to those chaste maidens, Agatha with her veil and tongs, and Lucy with the cord and her eyes on a silver dish ... Who is now to step forth on the cloudy floor of the high chamber in the city of Heaven and present the complaints of the downtrodden? Often the matters for which we seek redress are small, sometimes no more than a stubborn swelling in the armpit, though mostly it is by our fellow men that we are oppressed and ill-treated, both in flesh and in spirit ... He who has been flogged and starved and flogged again for trying feebly to procure food, and flogged yet again, this time much longer and harder because the name of Saint Dismas, protector of prisoners, came to lips bloody from a slit tongue; he is proof that in his defencelessness a cruelly beaten man needs the help of an intercessor in Heaven ... But, saddest of all, the very reason the man is in prison is due to his belief in the intercession of which he has been deprived ... Out of sight does not mean out of mind, however ... Saint Thorlákur still walks among his poverty-stricken countrymen and they still call on him to mention their names when he stands under the cascade of light that streams from Christ's four nail wounds and the hole in his side and from his battered head where the thorns pierced the skin to the bone ... But only those who have learnt the tongue of angels can tell how one's name will sound in the language of light ... So there is little to be gained by craning one's neck to the skies and combining one's name with prayers; that twittering will be of no more use than the croaking of a soulless Great Auk if there is no intercessor up there to interpret the mortal name of the one who prays and translate it into the language of Heaven ... We need the glorious Saint Thorlákur and Gudmundur the Good to translate the names of us poor sinners for the wondrous race above ... My name is Jónas Pálmason in Icelandic, Jonas Palmesen in Danish, Jahn Palmsohn in German, Jonah Palmson in English, and could be Johannes Palmensis in Latin, but what I am called in the language of eternity I will not learn until Doomsday ... I hope the call comes from above, because it is also said that everyone has another name in hell and I will be damned if I ever want to learn what they call me in that hideous place ... Ah, but you, sandpiper, have nothing to fear, for you have no name besides what people call you at any given moment, and those are all earthly names ... Heaven only has room for good men ... I suppose I will miss you when I get there ... Yes, just as those with the second sight can sense the presence of elves in the landscape despite never having set eyes on them, so true souls can experience the presence of the saints, despite the fact that the Church has been stripped of their images ...

—

JERUSALEM HADDOCK: *nine ells long, the fairest of all fish, with a girth almost equal to that of a flounder. Its flesh is sweet and exudes a great pile of fine, handsome butter in the dish, especially when chilled over night. One such fish was cut off by low tide with some trout in a river estuary on Skardsströnd, but no one dared to taste it until I did, who knew it well.*

—

My grandmother once said to her husband: 'Let little Master Nosy come with us this evening to see the Peter Lamb ...' For they still kept up the custom of dedicating the first lamb of summer to Saint Peter ... It was the Feast of the Assumption of Mary, the day on which the Virgin Mary at the end of her life rose from Earth to Heaven like the scent of a lily blossom, encountering on her way Our Lord Jesus Christ who, for love of his mother, stepped down from his throne, descending halfway from the sublime to the corporeal sphere, bringing with him a choir of angels to make the occasion more festive. He has not come near the mortal world since, but on that occasion he embraced the soul of the Holy Virgin and escorted her to the glories of Heaven ... And the old couple, my grandparents, had long been in the custom of visiting the lamb in honour of these events ... In truth, they seized every opportunity to visit it, though always after I had gone to bed, but I had never been surprised by their charity towards this motherless creature, taking it for granted that they were as kind to other orphans as they were to me ... After supper, Grandmother took me to my room and told me to put on my finest clothes ... I obeyed, and she did the same ... Then she made the sign of the cross over me and recited every five-year-old's favourite prayer about Mary:

Mary went to church,
met a holy cross,
wore a key on her belt,
to unlock Heaven ...
Almighty God and Peter
were singing there from books:
We shall go in summer
to visit our holy relics ...
Please God, make the sun shine
on that fair hill,
where Mary milked her cow ...

Then she took me by the hand and off we went to see the Peter Lamb ... But when we went round the back of the farm buildings to meet Grandfather, I was met by an extraordinary sight ... All the farmhands were gathered there, both men and women, as neatly combed and finely turned out as Grandmother and me ... They were waiting for us ... Grandfather Hákon led forward an old man with a nodding head and bent shoulders, clad in a cloak with the hood drawn down over his nose and holding a tall staff in his hand ... He set off towards the mountain with us following in his wake … Grandfather Hákon went first with the menfolk hard on his heels, carrying torches which instead of being lit were painted a fiery red at one end:

'So they won't be seen all over the district …' said one of the farmhands.

The women brought up the rear with us children … The man with the staff toiled up over the hayfields and no one but me fretted at his slow pace … I was wild with excitement to see the lamb … My grandmother kept a firm hold of my hand and I responded by dragging her along with all my might, leaning almost horizontally with the effort like a badly trained dog on a leash, but she would not be hurried … I thought the lamb must be one of the most remarkable creations on earth, given all this effort to make the visit so ceremonious and yet so secret … Ceremonious, for the people sang under the torches; secret, because the torches could not be lit and the singing was muted so as not to be heard beyond the procession … It was the seventh day of August and the summer nights were still light, though the shadow of the mountain had begun to turn blue in the evening and a stronger scent rose from the dewy grass of the farm mound in the morning … But the grassy farm knoll was not the only such mound in the world ... When I saw where the procession was heading, I abruptly slackened my hold on my grandmother's hand and pressed close to her skirts instead ... Before us was a hummock known as the Mary Mound, near which we children had been strictly warned not to play our noisy games ... We were told that it was the abode of the hidden people, who protected their home with magic spells ... These warnings were invariably accompanied by tales of rash youths who in their eagerness to show off had advanced boldly into battle against the mound dwellers ... All these youths lost their wits and ended their days tethered in stalls, lowing with the cattle ... Some of the older children had heard human lowing of this kind on their travels to distant lands, such as the next farm but one in the valley, or even further afield, the farm beyond that, and I used to shudder when they mimicked the sound of these half-men ... Now I leant backwards as I walked and dug in my heels, for from what I could tell the procession was headed to that very spot, the dreaded Mary Mound, where men went mad and were turned into beasts ... How come they kept the Peter Lamb there of all places? Why on earth would they put the blessed little beast in such peril? And what might the lamb not turn into if it happened to graze on the mound and fall foul of the spells of the malevolent unseen power? My imagination gave birth to a monster as huge as the dreadful mound itself ... A hairy sack that rolled inexorably along, dragging with it everything in its path ... Man and beast alike were ensnared in the wet tangles of its wool and pulled inwards to the corpse-pale flesh which was covered all over with yellow sheep's eyes, a coffin worm writhing in every one ... That would be the last thing I saw before the monster rolled another ring around itself and crushed me on a rock ... The material for this nightmarish vision was derived from the bloated carcass of a drowned ram that the older children had shown me at Hraunlón earlier that summer ... I cried out:

'I don't want to see the lamb!'

And dropped into the grass ... My grandmother jerked me briskly to my feet and pressed me close to her side without once breaking the rhythm of her stride or song ... There was no escaping ... For the remainder of the march I kept silent while the monster writhed and rolled and tumbled in my imagination ... When the procession reached the Mary Mound, the crowd gathered in its lee so as not to be seen from the other farms ... I had expected the Peter Lamb to greet us, bleating hungrily as is the custom of hand-reared lambs, but there was nothing here apart from the mound ... The crowd fell to their knees and clasped their hands, all except Grandfather Hákon, the old man in the hooded cloak and two farm workers; I myself naturally copied my grandmother's every move ... Peeping over my clasped fingers, I cast around for the lamb ... Instead I saw the farmhands remove spades from under their coats and, on my grandfather's orders, start to break soil on the mound ... They inserted the spades into gaps between the tussocks and sliced the turf crosswise, top and bottom, then down the slope from the middle of the upper cut to the middle of the lower one, until it resembled nothing so much as a pair of church doors as tall as a man ... Now each of the farmhands stuck his spade deep under a door, thereby loosening the turf from the soil ... After this, they peeled aside the doors, laying them back on the slope on either side like the panels of an altarpiece, revealing a rectangle filled with black earth ... I was deeply unimpressed by my grandfather's foolhardiness and could not understand why the good man should amuse himself by disturbing the peace of the cruel forces that dwelt in the Mary Mound, but then things took a turn for the worse ... Grandfather fetched from his pouch a thick hog-bristle brush and began to sweep it along the soil at head height ... I squeezed my eyes shut and pressed my forehead against my clasped hands: the spirits would not like this ... At that moment I heard a new sound: the gentle clacking of wooden beads ... Rosaries dropped from the sleeves of the people in the crowd and they began to tell them with sighs and moans, calling forth in my breast a mixture of laughter and anguish which I had never before realised could exist in the same place ... The brush whisked in my grandfather Hákon's hand ... The man in the cloak drew back his hood and at last I could glimpse something of his face: nose and eyes ... a tuft of hair on the nose, the blue eyes vacant ... Thrusting his staff into the spongy ground, he leant on it with his left hand while producing a small book from his scrip with his right ... The brush sent the last crumbs of the thin layer of earth whirling away to reveal underneath a layer of mottled sand from the seashore ... Grandfather wielded the brush on the sand with the same dexterity, working faster the deeper down he got ... Meanwhile, in a reassuring and unexpectedly boyish voice, the hairy-nosed, poached-eyed man with the staff began to read aloud from the little volume that lay open in his hand, without once looking at it:

'*Transitus Mariae* ... On the day when the glorious Queen of Heaven and Earth, the Holy Mary, passed away, all the Lord's apostles were present ... And wise authorities tell us that wherever each of the apostles had been standing previously, he was raised from there by angelic power and set down on the spot where the Holy Mary died ... For God's angel was sent by the Lord to raise up each of the apostles and carry him many days' journey through the air in the winking of an eye to bring him to this place ...'

I had abandoned any attempt to understand what the grown-ups were up to ... But of one thing I was sure: if you had to go through all this fuss just to set eyes on the Peter Lamb, then I was bored to death by the whole affair and determined to refuse any further invitations to visit, should they be forthcoming ... I loosened my clasped hands, feeling the blood rushing to my fingers, and stretched and flexed them in the air ... Grandmother gripped my skinny arm hard with a low cry ... I lost my temper with her since I had done nothing to deserve such rough treatment and was about to strike off the hand that crushed my arm so mercilessly ... But at that moment other people in the crowd began to emit similarly muffled cries ... Yes, it must be starting: the evil spirits were entering the people and without warning each would turn on his neighbour, bellowing and beating, crushing and tearing off fingers, noses and ears ... With a wail, I sprang to my feet ... Experience had taught me that the best course was to run to my grandfather Hákon, but if the world was turning topsy-turvy, he must surely become the most fearsome ogre of all, so I made up my mind to run off alone into the blue ...

'Wise men say that God had previously revealed to his apostles that they would all, on the day that the glorious Holy Mother passed away, gather in the valley known as *Vallis Josaphat* ...' intoned the old man.

I could not move an inch ... We were in the thick of the crowd, my grandmother and I ... When the homilist fell silent I heard Grandfather Hákon say:

'Come forth in jubilation, O Holy Mary, Mother of God, nursemaid of our Lord Jesus Christ!'

This did not sound like very monstrous talk to me so I plucked up the courage to look in his direction ... The brush twirled as before in his hand, but where there had been sand there now peeped forth the finely shaped tip of a nose made of painted wood, then ruddy cheeks, and with the next swirl of the brush appeared the celestial blue eyes, turned heavenwards, of God's Holy Mother ... The third swirl swept all the sand from her countenance and the fourth dislodged it, causing it to trickle like water to her feet, revealing her robed body ... My grandmother began to weep ... For, as I understood later, it was a long time since she had last set eyes on the Holy Virgin, the lady who had given her strength through all the years of childbirth, childrearing and housekeeping ... Her confidante in every trifling feminine concern that comes of being made not in the image of the Creator but in the image of an image, made from the substance of the male who was himself moulded from the earthly clay which became visible when the word fell from the lips of the Maker ... Upon which He took the substance in His palm and made from it ever smaller worlds until He made woman and all that she contains within ... The Holy Virgin knew women's insides better than any other, being herself a daughter of Eve; the most perfect of her line, but a mortal woman nonetheless ... Until the apostles saw her rise from her grave like a silver cloud which rose higher and higher until the Saviour floated to meet it, reaching a hand into the clouds and whisking his mother up to highest Heaven ... Now she sits crowned at his side, pleading the cause of mortal women ... It transpired that Our Lady was not the only statue in the elf-mound ... For here the images of the holy saints, carved, cast and painted, from our own and our neighbouring districts had been preserved when twilight fell over the land like snow, like ash from the infernal lava-spewing Mount Hekla that is fatal to any livestock that have not been brought into shelter ... For what are we but your flock, O Lord? We face the same perils as the cattle, sheep and geese that graze on grass turned an acrid black by the disaster ... That is why your flock has hidden its salvation underground, and from there draws its strength, acting in secret while celebrating in its heart, until the rule of the usurpers has come to an end and the libertine hordes lie with their innards burst open like young rats that have gorged themselves in the tallow barrel ... From this fair meeting with the Virgin in the Mary Mound, little Master Nosy's childish mind became gripped with the conviction that every mound, knoll and bump in the landscape concealed heavenly wonders ... Shortly before his death, my grandfather Hákon entrusted to me, then twenty-three years old, the instructions that showed where the True Believers had buried their saints ... This later became my passport to the fortress of learning that is Hólar ... There I exchanged the instructions for the schooling and priestly education of my son, Reverend Pálmi Gudmundur Jónasson ... Not that he has had much joy of being the son of Jónas the Learned, but the poor fellow obtained his place at Hólar because I knew the hiding places of those who had escaped the twilight portents, though that was not all I had to pay towards his keep: there was also the piece of paper proving Sheriff Ari of Ögur's treasonous dealings, that is, the contract he made with the Spaniards over the harpooning of whales, in defiance of his monarch's strict edict banning foreign ships from entering Icelandic waters, which referred to the captains who sailed to these shores as 'filthy thieves' ...

—

SHELL-HEAD, *or* **HUMPBACK WHALE:** *has shells and barnacles covering most of its head. Wherever the water is deep enough it rubs itself against barnacle-encrusted rocks. Of all the inedible whales, this is the greatest* *scourge of ships and men, for it will charge at boats and smash them in two with its fins, flippers or tail. At times it will block men's course, so they have no alternative but to collide with it. Upon which it will cast the ship high in the air if it can, and pick off everyone on board, unless men succeed in dodging so that it misjudges and charges past. However, the sound of an iron file is insupportable to it, causing it to go mad or kill itself. On hearing the sound of a thin piece of iron, about the size of a saw, being rasped against the gunwale using a large file, the humpback will be repulsed and flee or, if shallows are to be found nearby, take its own life by running aground. It contains a good deal of blubber and its short baleen makes fine runners for sledges. The humpback can grow to some sixty ells long.*

—

Yes, strutting sandpiper, your footprints in the sandy beach are your handwriting; thus you write your ephemeral tales and reports of what you have seen on your short-winged travels ... I learnt to form letters and illuminate capitals in the scriptorium in my grandfather's house, where I was entrusted with the copying and compilation of books ... These were minor works at first, timeless neither in content nor in execution ... A ballad or two and verses to entertain the traveller; handy little books containing instructions on how to cook tasty dishes; prayer books, and workbooks in which to preserve illustrations found in borrowed tomes but left out of the copies due to lack of space or else because they were out of fashion or contravened the new Church law ... I also copied the diagrams of anatomy in books of healing which showed mankind as we are: our form, the places where the flesh hugs the bone or swells out, all according to how the Creator's hand moulded our substance like clay ... Since the old women in country kitchens would no longer allow me to fumble their bodies, I collected in one volume everything I could find about healing the principal maladies afflicting the female anatomy ... There in alphabetical order you could find every kind of blockage, disorder of the blood, fever and chill, or swelling of their vitals or upper body ... Between these I copied out old prayers to the Virgin Mary and appeals to those saints who had proved most efficacious in curing the Icelandic belly, together with exorcisms and similar invocations of white magic to aid in the battle against the wiles of demons and other horrid sprites ... The bulk of this material was copied from the leechbook of the good Bishop Jón Halldórsson, and patients regarded it as an honour to hear that reverend man's wise counsel vying with the boiling of the kettle, the sucking of the chimney, the crackling of the lamps and the crunching of the gravel floor. They used to exclaim that it was as if the Lord Bishop himself had descended to the sooty kitchen to heal them ... In other words, I held to my course when it came to the healing of female disorders and the collection of ravens' heads ... But the leechbook would later land me in such desperate straits that I will never again be able to return to society but am fated instead to sit here talking nonsense to birds ... Having burnt one man, they were eager to burn more ... 'Schoolmaster of Necromancy' they called me when I helped some lads copy the leechbook and pronounce the names of the holy women who are addressed in the invocations ... Those hypocritical jackals would have burnt me too if the ladies I cured with the help of the late bishop had opened their mouths ... But no, they kept mum out of gratitude for my care ... Yet although my body hair was not singed on their bonfire, I felt the heat of the animosity they bear towards me, the vindictive nature that drives a man to destroy his neighbour in a fire as if he were a banned book ... For what is the difference? Every book is imbued with the human spirit ... They knew that, the sooty guardians of the kitchen hearths, when they claimed to hear the bishop's voice in the descriptions of their maladies and fell on their knees, only to jump up with reproaches when they heard that I had compiled the text myself ... It was all in fun ... And yet ... I would not dream of comparing myself to Bishop Jón, any more than it would cross your mind, sandpiper, to liken the puff of air from your short wings to the whoosh from an eagle's flight ... To watch a book burn ... My eyes are smarting ... In the conflagration I hear the breath of the man who composed the text, and the breath of the man who formed the words, one after the other, and the breath of the man who reads it ... I hear this trinity breathing as one and the same being, steadily in and out, until the fire consumes the breath from their lungs, disbanding the fellowship of those whom the book nurtured, like the soil that brings forth different plants ... And many were the intertwined souls that burnt at Helgafell when the old monastery library was cast on the bonfire, along with the few holy relics and statues that had not already been destroyed ... Alas, I was there! ... What could my puny strength achieve when set against the giant pyre that raged like three volcanic craters, so great was the heat from that diabolical act? ... And who should have been the Royal Incendiary of the first pyre, the Master Incendiary of the second pyre, the Grim Incendiary of the third? He whose duty it was to take the lead in the spiritual education of the flock in that parish, Reverend Sigurdur Pétursson, a young man who had recently taken up the living there ... A sunny countenance, spare of flesh, nimble in his movements and loving to his wife and the child she bore under her belt ... They had occupied the living for only four months when he lost his mind ... which was seventeen days before he ordered the burning ... That day Reverend Sigurdur awoke before anyone else, already raving ... He ran in his nightshirt to the library, locked himself in and began hurling the books higgledy-piggledy on the floor ... The servants watched aghast through the windows as he tore off his shift, flung himself on his back and rolled around on the books like a flea-bitten stray in the farmyard ... Howling, he seized the writings at random, laid them on his naked flesh and rubbed them against himself, up and down, up and down, in a sinful fashion ... But when he started ripping pages from the books and shoving them into his bodily orifices, the servants, afraid that he would choke himself, broke down the door ... They overpowered the minister and tied him to his bed ... The source of his madness was traced to a thumb-sized statue carved of whale ivory, supposedly representing Saint Barbara with her tower, which the minister's young wife had found among the old clutter belonging to the monks and intended to use as a bogeyman for the unborn child ... She had been toying with this object, which had probably been carved by some newly baptised Greenlander, while sitting on the bed in the couple's room and had inadvertently pushed it under her husband's pillow ... So Reverend Sigurdur had been sleeping on it the night he went mad ... When he was released from his bed-prison seventeen days later, however, the parson's mind was sharper and more lucid than ever before ... He ordered his sexton to clear out the library, pile the heretical collection in a heap in the field and build three bonfires with the books, which he then set alight himself ... Providence guided me to Helgafell that day ... I was meant to witness the tragedy ... I was on my way to Stadarstadur to paint an altarpiece that I had carved earlier that winter ... Seeing a pall of smoke over Helgafell as if the very hill were on fire, I gave in to curiosity and headed for the parsonage ... Had I been able to fly like a bird, I might have made do with lifting myself over the hill to see what was causing the smoke ... But no, I covered the whole distance on foot, arriving to find the fire at its height and, falling on my knees before it, I wept ... That day Jónas 'the Learned' sank to new depths of ignominy in the eyes of his fellow men ... But they did not see what I saw ... Or if they did see, they did not understand what was happening before their eyes ... When the bonfire in the middle, the largest, breathed its last, admitting a rush of air to the embers like a thousand devils all racing in single file down the same pipe, there was a great crack of thunder from the pyre ... Everyone jumped – there was not supposed to be any gunpowder in the fire ... While they were exchanging astonished glances, I kept my gaze fixed on the flames ... I saw an open book rise from the pyre and float over the blazing pile ... It appeared to be quite intact, the spine facing down, the pages spreading like wings

... In an instant it glowed a dazzling white ... And the parson's youngest daughter cried out in a high voice:

'Baba, see de birdy!'

Next moment the book exploded in a shower of sparks ... And the heat blew them to heaven ... A year later Reverend Sigurdur rowed out in a boat to collect down and eggs from a small island in Lake Helgafell with two of his siblings to help ... By then he had become so arrogant in spiritual matters that he did not give a fig for the enchantment under which the island was said to lie ... But on that trip his boat was holed in the middle and all three of them drowned ... O little bird, do not let Man's innumerable acts of wickedness weary you into fluttering too close to their bonfires, lest your flight feathers be singed ... Indeed, we must look to our wits, brother Jeremiah ...

—

BLUEBOTTLE: *lays oblong eggs from which maggots hatch; if they are kept in a bull's horn, come the spring they will turn into flies which the trout enjoys. The bluebottle is fat and as thick as a man's thumb.*

II

(Summer Solstice, 1636)

Last winter I was as solitary as Adam in his first year in Paradise, though the island in winter is nothing like that delightful place. It is cold and bleak and one does not venture out of doors except to empty one's chamber pot, and not properly even then; one merely opens the door a crack, just wide enough for the pot. I was more like a wretched mouse in its hole than a man created in God's image. As little and hunched as the rat's cousin, not ramrod straight, proudly surveying my domain like Adam. Ah, yes, Adam was tall and held his head high. That way he could see over the whole world, for he was bigger and heavier than his living descendants, just under thirty yards in height, and with such a head of hair that his locks cascaded like a waterfall over his loins. He was the largest living creature that God had created from earthly clay. And all through that year as he walked the earth alone, his massive body was being fired and glazed by the sun like clay in an oven. All growth was new: the trees put down roots, sprouted, then dropped their leaves and stood naked for the first time. The swans rose honking from the moorland tarns and heard their own voices for the first time. The lily opened her flowers and her perfume filled the air for the first time. The bee alighted on the dwarf fireweed and quenched her thirst with fresh honey before buzzing in flight to the next flower cup. It had never happened before. Everything was new to the eyes of the man and he was entirely new to himself. Moulded by the Master from the four elements, as they combine in the earth, he was closer to his origins now than he ever would be again. His blood was still diluted with seawater, there was gravel in his flesh, roots crept along his sinews and muscles, the seed that quickened to life in his testicles was thick as spider silk and foamy as sea spume. Thus he strode across the world and wherever he looked he saw to the ends of the Earth. At night the starry sky turned over his head, an ever-moving, twinkling, living picture show, and his childish eyes began at once to draw lines between the points of light as he sought there for parallels to the things that he perceived on his journeys by day: a swan, a ram, a snake. By day the blazing orb of the sun floated over his head and its heat drew the sweat from his skin. On the longest day of the world's first year Adam grew so hot that the sweat broke out all over him and ran in torrents down his colossal trunk. Most of the liquid was absorbed by the golden mane that cloaked his body, and to wring the wetness from his hair Adam shook himself as he had seen the dog do – alone of all beasts this creature had taken to following him wherever he went – but in spite of such tricks the sweat continued to spring from its human source. Adam bent his head and cupped his hands to catch the liquid that poured down his forehead and fell like rain from his brow. He watched the bowl fill and the level of the salty water rising fast, before long reaching his thumb and forefinger, but for a moment before it flowed over the sides, its surface grew still and Adam saw a wondrous sight in the mirror of his hands: he saw himself. Thirst had not yet driven him to the waters, he did not yet know hunger, for a year was no more than an hour to the immortal man. And so he did not know himself in the eyes that gazed at him from the pool of sweat, did not recognise the smooth, glowing face that framed them, nor the nose that separated them. Shrieking with fright, Adam threw up his hands. When he dared to look back at where the face had appeared there were no more eyes to be seen, the mirror had shattered into countless drops, and although he collected more sweat in his palms the surface was never again smooth enough to show a whole picture, for agitation made his hands tremble too much. After a while he gave up and stood without moving, staring blankly into space, his arms hanging idly at his sides. The sun descended in the sky and he felt her heat moving from his neck to his shoulders, from where she began her journey down his long spine. And then yet another wonder occurred, a phenomenon which he would hardly have noticed had the novel sight earlier that day not opened his eyes to the possibility that the visible world had more to it than that which is solidly present; why, from his feet grew a creature which seemed to originate in himself. At first it was nothing but a faint pool, though not shaped at all like a pool, and for a while he thought that this too was liquid pouring from his body, but by the time the patch of sunshine on his spine had settled lukewarm in the small of his back, the phenomenon had acquired a familiar form: a flat head, broad shoulders and a thick trunk with long arms and short legs. Adam started back: it resembled nothing so much as the apes that lived in the southern part of the garden. In contrast to the dogs, these creatures treated him with contempt, scowling and grimacing whenever he came near. He did not know then that these grotesque half-men were put on Earth by the Creator so that he would recognise himself in them when he fell into sin. Ah, but there was still a long time to pass before the day when in their distorted faces he would see his own visage in pride, envy, rage, idleness, lechery, covetousness or gluttony. Free from sin as he was, Adam did not understand the taunt, seeing them only as mischievous, hairy creatures, and often wondered why they were allowed to exist. But as the first man started back, so the dark creature moved backwards with him, following close, pursuing him as if sewn to his feet, and when he finally straightened his back after trying to shake it off, trying in vain to tear its feet from his own, it had grown so long that it was almost as tall as himself. He had often lain on his back, feeling his own limbs, stroking from his upper arm down to his hand and along each finger to the tip, and in the same way his hands travelled down his thighs and calves to his toes – and beyond. Thus Adam was aware of the general form of his body, and in the dark patch that lay at his feet he saw for the first time a creature that resembled himself. At that moment his solitude was revealed to him, loneliness pierced his childish soul: all around him he saw pairs standing in the meadow: the lions and the sheep, the lizards and the tortoises, and in the waters the walruses and the whales, the flounders and the salmon, while above flew two swans and two eagles, and in the birch scrub a pair of snow buntings puffed out their breasts and sang of the joys of coupledom. Adam gazed out over the wide world; could it be that he had overlooked his other half? No, on his journeys around the Earth he had peered under every stone, groped inside every crevice, turned over every clump of seaweed; there was nothing to be found that resembled him. Just as disappointment threatened to flare up inside him, bringing with it a sinful sense of ingratitude towards the Creator, his eyes happened to fall on the image on the ground and a still stronger sensation seized hold of his mind, yes, and body too. Now it so happened that when this being found its way out of Adam's soles he was standing on the margin between land and sea, on sandy ground full of dips and hollows, dimpled and gently rounded. The image on the ground was thus much softer than him in form, the dips and swellings adding curves to its hips and breast. Yes, the feeling that gripped his mind also gripped his body. The limb between his legs swelled, reared up and jutted forwards, like the strong arm of an army commander ordering his troops into battle: 'Onwards to victory!' And without further ado Adam obeyed the command of his powerfully raised limb. He cast himself over the creature, thrusting his limb between its legs, deep into the sandy soil, pumping on top of it until a great, thick stream of sperm spurted from his body with the force of a tidal wave crashing against a cliff forty fathoms high. The climax shattered the rainbow on the inside of his eyelids, each colour shooting out into the void like a meteor, sometimes violet, sometimes blue as water, sometimes yellow as the sun, and the seed flowed into every cleft in the Earth's crust, every crack in the rocks, every groove and fissure in the crystals, every hole in the soil. Thus Adam fertilised the underworld by lying with his own shadow. From this act sprang the race that dwells in the dark worlds underground. Was it thrice three hundred thousand that quickened to life on that single occasion? Is that the reason why wherever mankind settles, he is preceded by a vast horde of invisible beings in mounds and hillocks, crags and mountains? But the Creator saw that this would not do: what an abhorrent thought that man should be filled with lust for his own shadow, let alone that from him should spring such a legion of offspring every time he lay with the earth. Before long, there would be no room for the mass of earth-dwellers in the darkness and they would burst forth with the same force as the sperm from their father's loins. So the first thing the Maker of Man did was to deprive Adam of his shadow until he had found a solution to the problem. And while Adam rushed around the realm of the Earth, seeking an object for his lechery – bellowing with lust, leading a chorus of howling dogs that followed his every step – the Maker of the World invented woman, taking care to form her belly in such a way that it could hold no more than three human embryos at a time. Yes, and their species would shrink by an inch with every generation until man was not much taller than the ignorant son of Adam who sits here on the shore with his misshapen shadow, putting down these thoughts in words.

—

Sun, I thank you for obeying the Almighty Creator's call and lengthening your course across the sky in summer. Were it not for this, we who live up here on this unlovely splat of lava in the far north of the globe would go stark, staring mad – every last one of us. For so it has been arranged for us that for one quarter of the year the sky is always light, for another quarter it is always dark, and for the other two it is passable. Such are our seasons. In the perpetual light of high summer one has leisure to contemplate the terrible black chill that is the season we call winter, and all the evil that it brings. After such thoughts one sits and turns one's face to the sky, closing one's eyes and letting the blueness fill one with the illusion that it will always be so, or at most that the sky will flush like the cheek of a bashful boy but never grow dark again. For there is need of light when one's memories are dark, as I know to my cost. All day I have been prey to ugly, dismal thoughts. Yet I have so much to rejoice over: the warm sunny weather, the broad vista, the gentle cries of the birds and the pups calling from the seal colony, sounding for all the world like human babes. And my wife, Sigrídur Thórólfsdóttir, is with me. The poor dear woman who thought she was embarking on the dance of life with a reasonably affluent and industrious man when she married me. Thirty-five years later she knows better. They brought her to me this spring, saying that she was restless with longing to see me, the poor soul. Yes, Sigga is a sad wretch, a match for that sad wretch Jónas. I thought her coming would lighten my life, that less time would be wasted on worrying about my belly, and that I would instead have more leisure to devote to pondering matters of importance, to fixing them in my mind. For they stick better if I have someone to lecture to. But these days Sigrídur gets all cross and perverse when I try to impart my ideas, and tempers are lost.

'There he goes again!' she says, turning away as if I have produced a stream of piss. I make no attempt to respond. Yet what ensues is inevitable:

'That's the sort of nonsense that landed us here in the first place.'

What she says is true, though she should know better than to call it nonsense; it would be more correct to say that it was my intellectual gifts that marooned us here. Or rather, exiled *me* here; it was her decision to make them row her over to share my fate. Poor woman. But it is probably the lesser of two evils to be the wife of Jónas and share a barren rock with him than to live among strangers. Or so I gathered from the way people spoke to her on the mainland. The saddest thing for me is that her loyalty is misplaced. I have done this woman nothing but harm. She was opposed to my heeding the summons of Wizard-Láfi Thórdarson, alias the specialist and poet Thórólfur, when he asked me to go out west with him and exorcise the troublesome ghost. For that was the beginning of my misfortunes. That is how we came to lose everything. How did our paths cross? It was during the eclipse of the sun, if I remember right. I do not dare ask her; women think men ought to remember that sort of thing. Last time she was scolding me for my madcap ideas, I asked her why she had come back to me if not to take up the thread where we left off when I had to crawl alone into hiding due to the persecution by the Nightwolf and Sheriff Ari of myself Jónas the Learned and my son Reverend Pálmi. Indeed, why was she here if not to assist me in my investigations into the workings of the universe? For that is how it used to be. Now it is as if my enemies have given her the task of 'bringing me to my senses', as more than one, indeed several, of my tormentors call it. Yet that is not fair, for when I hinted as much the other day, she responded:

'If anyone knows there's no chance of bringing you to your senses by now, Jónas Pálmason, it's me.'

Sigga was the bonniest lass I had ever met. I first heard of her when a visitor told my grandfather

Hákon and me that they were having problems with a girl down at Bakki in Steingrímsfjord. She was moonstruck, but not like those familiar crazed fools who are best off begging. No, her lunacy rendered her calm and sensible, while at the same time obsessed with the light of the moon and its path across the firmament, its size and phases. When found to be missing from her bed, she was tracked down at last by the cowshed wall, thumb in the air, calculating how the moon's shadow had grown from the day before. And if she could lay hands on paper and writing materials, she would begin at once to scribble down numbers and lines. Indeed, the minister who was called to examine her said she seemed to possess a sound knowledge of arithmetic. However, she could not be persuaded to tell where she had acquired this learning, for she can hardly have got the hang of it alone and unaided, and the people of the house were pretty sure that some vagabond must have passed on the knowledge to her: 'In return for goodness knows what payment.' But her girlish head had been unable to cope with the arithmetic and she had lost her wits, as was proven by the fact that she had become enamoured of that work of nature, the moon, which invariably attracts an ailing mind. The perpetrator of this wicked deed was never found, though people suspected a failed student from Hólar, who had been expelled for striking the bishop with the Easter sacrament: one Thórólfur Thórdarson, known to all as 'Wizard-Láfi'. This was the first occasion on which Láfi was to play a fateful role in my life. For had he not so inadvertently led me and Sigga together, and had we not had him to thank for our meeting, she would never have been persuaded to allow me to go north to the Snjáfjöll coast to help him lay the ghost. In truth I had until now had little time for the female of the species, regarding the entire tribe as tedious and irksome company. No doubt the feeling was mutual: they were bored by my philosophising and I was bored by their talk of housekeeping, provisions, child-rearing and whatever they call all that futile business around which their lives revolve. Naturally people whispered that I was impotent with regard to women. What of it? The other bachelors need have no fear that I would compete with them for the wenches. Yet this did not prevent them from commissioning me to write poems ablaze with ardent feelings for the opposite sex. The girl from Bakki was not only of marriageable age but also rumoured to be interested in the heavenly bodies. That sounded promising. Well, I would not give up until I had set eyes on this paragon. It was in the spring of 1598, on the seventh of March. How do I remember? It was the spring when the eclipse sent both man and beast mad. When I arrived at Bakki I pretended to be passing through on my way to Hólar to present the bishop with a book that had long ago been removed from the episcopal seat, *ex libris* of that decapitated martyr of the True Faith, Bishop Jón Arason. It contained a handful of Greek fables by the wise author Aesop, translated into Latin and illustrated with comical pictures of witless beasts going about human business. A frivolous book from pagan Asia but a valid passport for my sightseeing trip to Bakki. I certainly had the book with me, in case anyone asked, and could show it to trustworthy types if required. I was received with generous hospitality, though the farm was in a state of mourning as the father of the householder had recently departed this life and his body was still lying in state upstairs. I behaved like any other visitor who merely happened to be passing along the fjord on the aforementioned business and had not at all come to catch a glimpse of the moonstruck girl. I was well provided for with food and drink. The good people found me entertaining and listened in silent pleasure to my poems and discursions on natural history, for I adapted my material as befitted a house where a corpse was lying in the parlour. And no one thought it odd that I should have business with the women in the kitchen as in former times. Nothing had changed in there; indeed, kings may come and kings may go but the kitchen hearth remains unchanged, with its fire, food and gossip. I assumed the moonstruck girl would have an errand there sooner or later, and while I was waiting I took a look up the skirts of a couple of old biddies, and fumbled another three, for they allowed me access again, never suspecting that I would be aroused by that touch – however much they themselves might enjoy it. I also pulled a rotten molar out of the eldest of them, who, to my astonishment, was none other than the woman who had teased me with her dirty talk a whole decade before. Alas, why does God allow the candle of worthless old hags to flicker, year in year out, for nine times nine years, while abruptly and without apparent mercy blowing out the newly kindled flames of one's own children? It is an ugly thought which everyone who has ever lost anyone has entertained, demanding in their despair, why him? Why her? Why not that one or that one, or that other? But I cannot help it. And I would not be surprised if the old crone is still alive now, a hundred and forty years old and convinced there is nothing more natural, though she is of no use to anyone and hardly a source of pleasure even to herself. Anyway, her tooth had no sooner been extracted than there was a great hubbub of raised voices and people began to pour out of the buildings. The old women and I were just scrambling to our feet when a farmhand burst into the kitchen and flung himself on all fours, screeching without pause as he pushed his way through the bundle of skirts:

'It's going out, I tell you, it's going out!'

—

OLEANDER: *a poisonous plant which grows by the Lagarfljót River, between Grænamó and Jórvíkurrimi. If livestock graze on it, they die instantly and their bodies swell up. If rubbed, oleander turns yellowish green in colour and feels somewhat moist to the touch.*

—

I first glimpsed my future wife by the will o' the wisp light of the eclipse. At the very moment when the sun was halved, Sigrídur captured my gaze with her eyes – eyes that were a haven of peace amidst the storm of madness that raged on the farm. For I was as bewildered as the dogs that howled, the cats that hissed, the ravens that crawled along the ground, the cows that wandered dazed in the fields. I was as unfortunate as the rest, as unmanned by dread of what catastrophe this eclipse might bring, what terrible tidings it might portend, what loss of life, what pestilence would now wash up from the sea on to our rock, what heresies, what insanity; indeed, I was as confounded as those who ran weeping round the yard or pressed their faces to the muddy paving slabs, tore off their clothes and any hair they could grab hold of, many vomiting in mid-prayer. Yes, I was so terrified that even the marrow of my smallest bones quivered like the wings of a hoverfly – for mankind was helpless, trapped in the midst of the scene that the Apostle Mark had painted in words and the ministers in their Good Friday sermons had branded on our minds as if with a red hot poker; the last hour of the Saviour's life, the ninth hour when darkness fell at noon, when in his torment he doubted the existence of the merciful Father. If even His favourite, ever-blessed son was filled with dread, how could we poor sinful humans fail to lose our minds with fear? And lose them we did, all except Sigrídur. From inside the farm came a shriek:

'A miracle! A miracle! He is risen again!'

Shortly afterwards three men burst out of the front door carrying the old man's body between them. They swung the corpse's mottled limbs back and forth until it appeared to be raising its wizened arms to heaven, its head thrown back, the jaw falling slackly open to reveal the swollen blue tongue for all to see. It did not take a great physician to realise that the old man was as thoroughly dead as he had been but a short time before. People now began to crowd around the threesome with their pathetic puppet. One held its neck and left arm, the second its waist and right arm, the third and strongest stood behind the corpse, throwing both his arms round the bloated belly and lifting it so that it appeared to be proceeding in little hops to the intended destination, which was the roof of the living quarters. Here is another manifestation of insanity: people are united in actions which they would neither have known how to do nor dreamt of doing until seized by madness. And afterwards they are none the wiser about how to perform those deeds that madness rendered easy. While the servants were forcing their way on to the roof with the old man's body, Sigrídur took me aside. She had already taken precautions to save me from being caught up in the pandemonium. Without taking her eyes off me she stepped forward and took my hand, and when my gaze seemed about to falter and return to the compellingly infectious behaviour of the others, she followed me, taking another small side-step so that I was looking at her, not them. Thus she lured me step by step into her state of serenity, until she could lead me away. Once we were a good distance from the farm, she told me that she had known a solar eclipse was due, not precisely when, of course, but that one was in the offing. I froze in my tracks, my mouth felt dry and a cold sweat broke out all over my body. Smiling at me, she told me to follow her and we passed out of sight of the farm buildings where the herd of lunatics was trampling the fallow winter turf of the gable, raising the cadaver aloft in silhouette against the grey sky. Once sheltered from view, she sat me down and took a seat facing me across a flat piece of ground. Having gathered some pebbles in her hand, she began to arrange them into a planetary model, laying the largest stone in the middle and calling it Earth, then placing next to it the moon and sun and five planets in a straight line away from them. After this, she began to move the heavenly bodies round the Earth according to their familiar orbits until the sun and moon stood face to face.

'Here there will be an eclipse of the moon.'

Using a slender heather stalk she drew rays extending from the sun to Earth, then showed how the Earth in this position must cast its shadow on the moon. Next she counted several times on her fingers, muttering the names of the months and diverse numbers. She was calculating when the next lunar eclipse would take place and told me the date.

'You'll see; wherever you are in the country you'll discover it's true – weather permitting.'

Now Sigrídur moved the pebbles once again, saying meanwhile in her bright girlish voice:

'On the other hand it's impossible to predict solar eclipses accurately, though we can assume one will take place after a certain period, more or less. I've been waiting a long time for this one.'

By this stage I was not so much listening to the words that fell from her lips as staring at the lips themselves, at their ever-changing shape. I moved closer to examine them better. Sigrídur stopped talking and, taking a piece of blue glass from her apron pocket, raised it to her eye and looked at the sun. The chirping of small birds was stilled, the baying of the dogs was silenced, the people on the turf roof ceased shaking the corpse, a hush descended on the countryside and I felt suddenly cold. High above the Earth the disc of the moon completed its shape on the orb of the sun and in the same instant something was completed inside me. Neither Sigrídur nor I looked up when the gable gave way with a loud crack beneath the weight of the corpse-bearers. Our courtship was one uninterrupted conversation about the origin of the stars, the nature of land and sea, the behaviour of beasts great and small, and although it was not conducted in Hebrew or in the angelic tongue as it was with Adam and Eve, it was nevertheless our hymn to Creation. We sat together into the early hours, investigating the delightful puzzles of light and shadow, such as what happens to the shadow of your hand when the shadow of mine falls upon it? Have they become one? Or has yours disappeared temporarily? And if so, where to? We could talk like this for days, but no more. She fell silent when my enemies, no longer content with abusing me, began their persecution of our son, Reverend Pálmi Gudmundur. The boy was stripped of his habit and his calling. He is now forced to wander from farm to farm like a beggar, his wife constantly with child, like his father – alas. It grieves me just as much as it does Sigrídur to know how little my resistance achieved.

—

DIACODUS: *this stone has many useful properties. If it is placed in water, a host of spirits appear in it, apparelled like men, and one may ask it to foretell the future. The stone has been found in Iceland. Exemplum: when we lived at Uppsandar my wife Sigrídur happened to be walking beside the sea at the place where the mountainous shore is known as Fellshraun. On a certain flat rock over which the waves broke, she spied something round floating in a pool. When she picked it up, she thought it looked like a stone with magic properties. There was a pink dot high up in the middle and it was girded about with crimson, while the part under water looked green. She took it over to another smaller pool and dropped it in. All at once she saw countless human shapes appear in the water. Seeming to remember that I had read of such a stone, she reacted quickly, intending to put it in her glove and bring it home to me. But before the diacodus could find its way into* *her mitten, it fell on the shingle with a sharp crack and instantly vanished from sight. Sigrídur would never tell me what she learnt from the spirits but I assume she must have asked them her fortune.*

—

Alas, how Sigga implored me not to go west to meet Thórólfur. Oh, how right she was when she said it was the demon of vanity that summoned me to do the deed. I wanted to enhance my renown, I said, so that more people would avail themselves of my services. Self-taught as I was, I had to prove myself by my actions. And the man who succeeds in laying a ghost so malevolent that it tans the hide of every person who goes near it, that man will be prized when the twilight portents get out of hand and call down the wrath of God on the libertine herd. I seem to remember saying something to this effect, to which she replied:

'But aren't the rams you're going to perform the deed for the very same that the Lord will strike down?'

And yet … That must have been later. She let me go anyway, since we owed our meeting to Sorcery-Láfi. It was on that journey west along the Snjáfjöll coast that the catalogue of images etched itself on my mind – the traveller's album that always stands open before my eyes when I compare the world of piety and good works evoked by my grandfather Hákon in his stories to that other world into which I was born: the world where good deeds count for nothing, while conceited bragging of one's own virtues is enough to purchase tyrants notorious throughout the land a seat at the footstool of the risen Christ. Their busy tongues labour in their jaws while the fruit withers on the vine. On my way west I followed the highway, the road trodden by the common populace on their comings and goings along the shores of this island, which, in common with other circles, has no beginning and no end. And the business that draws the ragged mob from one corner of the country to the other? To beg a bite to eat, of course. Or rags to wear. To feel the warmth of something other than their own hand. To experience compassion. To be a guest rather than a nuisance. To receive a small share of the gifts of the Earth. To have all this. Yes, to be a Christian among Christians, even if only for the brief duration of the major Church holidays. My journey took place shortly after Easter – a holiday that had lost its meaning now that Lent had been scorned and people ate whatever they could shovel into their mouths. Rotting shreds of meat festooned their teeth like Christmas decorations when they yawned during the Good Friday sermon, their gums swollen an angry red where they had begun to fester, yet they could not be bothered to pick their teeth, instead sucking and licking with the tips of their tongues, worrying at the nagging pain in the swollen lumps, sighing when the pus was forced out between their molars, bringing the piece of meat with it into the mouth where it became the gravy for their putrid banquet. But not everyone was fortunate enough to spend Easter with their mouths full of this kind of sweetmeat. God's lambs, Christ's lambs, Peter's lambs: once upon a time the bands of itinerant beggars knew where these sweetly named lambs were kept and what time of the year they might be visited. These poor hungry wretches moved right round the country, like the stars of heaven on a metal arc around a model of the Earth; ah yes, when Spitting-Sveinn shaded his eyes and looked in the direction of Gaulverjabær in the Flói district, or Peg-leg Sigurgeira stood in Eyjafjord, squinting to assure herself that it was not far to Laufás. Marked out by God as Easter fare or Christmas roast, the ceremoniously named lambs walked out to meet the needy, out of the barn, out of their fleeces, out of their skins, frolicsome, fat and juicy, and kept on walking though their flesh changed colour as it roasted, walked across the yard, lathered in their own melted fat, to await the guests at the crossroads, positioning themselves and rotating so that the guests could see for themselves the browned, muscular rump under its glaze of fat and the shoulder where the blood burst forth and ran down the spine. Then the lambs would skip off home to the farm, chased by the starving rabble with gaping mouths and bared teeth. In the yard the lambs would halt and look back over their shoulders at the wretched throng before shaking themselves as if they had just returned from a swim and spraying a great arc of fat which cascaded over the faces of the needy, who stuck out their tongues as they ran, like children chasing fat snowflakes as they fall, lapping up the rain of suet, scraping the film of grease from their eyes and cheeks. Once home the lambs were driven back inside the kitchen by the farmhands and cooks, and there they paced back and forth on the red-glowing grids which the fire licked merrily, and from their roasting throats came forth smoke and crackling bleats announcing that soon their happy task would be accomplished, soon their procession would be over and they would tread the boards of the long trestle table in the hall which housed the vagabonds, beggar women and their urchin spawn, and there the lambs would reach the end of their journey, there they would reach their final goal, there their duty to the Lord would be completed, for they would walk to the gaping mouths of the guests and shake themselves by their teeth until the golden-brown flesh loosed from their bones and the grease cascaded from the tongue down the throat. But this would not happen until Easter Day. Until then, Spitting-Sveinn and Peg-leg Sigurgeira would willingly fast with their Redeemer and eat dried fish with butter. There was happiness in that too: worship, participation in the earthly incarnation of the divinity. But by the time I went on my journey to Snjáfjöll those days were long gone. The barefoot brigade were no longer offered any victuals, whether it was a juicy leg of lamb dedicated to a saint or the skin of a dried haddock, or a roof over their heads or gloves for their chapped hands. Far from it. Now the libertine life was all, and everything a man acquired belonged to him and his kin alone. The rest could eat dirt. And they did. As I began to near the manor farm which used to be governed by God's almanac, I was met by an abominable sight: the bodies of beggars lying beside the road, weathered sacks of skin stretched over the bones of adults and children. Ravens and foxes had gnawed at their heads and hands, clawed and torn off their rags and dined on their meagre pauper's flesh. Yes, there you have it, whether you are high-born or lowly, a stout figure or a whip-thin emaciated wretch, when your time on Earth is over you will be nothing but a sack of skin, emptied of its contents: the soul will have departed and without it you will be nothing but a leather bag of bones.

—

> **SEA MONSTER:** *of sea monsters I will say nothing, for I have not read much about them, though I had seen a fair number until they disappeared during the great winter of famine, Anno Domini 1602, the winter that men of the West Fjords refer to as 'Torment' and others as 'Cudgel'.*

—

Sorcery-Láfi was neither whip-thin nor starving. He was short of leg and wide of hip, with a premature stoop, plump cheeks, lively watery blue eyes set in a round head and black hair that always looked wet, as if newly washed, from the fish-liver oil he dressed it with. He was so light of heart that his behaviour bordered on the idiotic. He was forever clicking his fingers and whistling as he walked, spinning suddenly on his heel, clapping his hands together and declaring:

'Heigh-ho, the sun and snow!'

Or some other such harmless nonsense. He was an amusing fellow, with a poetic tongue that served him well in his dealings with the squires out west, helping him to ingratiate himself and sell them his services, which consisted mainly of escorting them on journeys, telling them jokes and composing comic verses whenever the opportunity arose. Also preparing hot poultices for their swellings, bleeding them, trimming their beards and singeing the hairs from their ears. And last but not least, being alert to the possible scheming of rogues who might pay witches to raise demon familiars against them. Now Láfi had summoned me to help him lay a ghost which had been running riot in the coastal district of Snjáfjöll. The spirit was so devious that Láfi had given up trying to tackle it on his own. It was thought to be the shade of a parson's son who had been cruelly treated by his father and stepmother, beaten and mocked and finally forced out in a violent storm to bring home some sheep that were in fact quite snug in a cave on the mountain above the farm. Since the shepherd had given up trying to drive them home, the parson put pressure on his son to prove himself the better man. It was not unkindly meant: both shepherd and parson's son happened to have their eye on the same maidservant, and it was clear to all that she preferred the shepherd, who had the stronger grip and the bushier whiskers. The parson's son, on the other hand, was a delicate youth who minced rather than walked, as unfit for physical work as he was for spiritual labours. He had been deeply attached to his late mother and used to help her with the needlework. Now he was wrapped up in layer upon layer of coats, with sturdy boots on his feet, a hat of polar-bear skin on his head and an iron-shod staff lashed to his right hand. Thus equipped, he set out on tiptoe over the hard-frozen snow. Onlookers made fun of his ridiculous high-stepping gait as it took him the best part of a day to clamber up to the top of the slopes, a point any other man could have reached in two hours. There he vanished from view and shortly afterwards fell over a cliff, broke his leg in three places and died of exposure. It was not long, however, before he returned to wreak vengeance on his father and neighbours, becoming the most palpable ghost ever to haunt the district; many were injured by his blows and stone-throwing when he ambushed them in the winter darkness. If a lamp went out in the living room during supper, he would have licked out all the bowls by the time it was re-lit. But it was no better when he satisfied himself merely with pinching women in the crotch and kicking men in the balls, hoping by this to castrate the district until it fell into dereliction. He had given Láfi such an almighty kick in the groin that one of his testicles had been squashed flat like a blueberry between the teeth, as I was permitted to see and feel for myself. Yet Láfi's attempts to exorcise the phantom parson's son had not been entirely unsuccessful. For the first few months afterwards the ghost had kept a low profile, hardly laying a finger on anyone, though he could be heard from time to time howling down the kitchen chimney. But when summer came round and the ghost was discovered to have pushed a shepherd boy flat on his face and torn off his breeches, Láfi admitted defeat: a ghoul that did not require the cover of darkness to commit its foul deeds was beyond his powers. So here I was, come to help him lay its body in the grave – where the spirit departed after that was not within our power to decide. Láfi was to be paid a fee for the ghost-hunt, and this he would share with me. We were well provided with food and drink and made tolerably comfortable at the parsonage of Stadur. But as the weather was exceptionally fine that year, we slept outside for most of the summer, using a tent that Láfi had acquired from a Spanish whaler. We began our quest by travelling from farm to farm, enquiring whether the spook had been there and, if so, how it had behaved. We were given a warm welcome and in return entertained the locals with our ballads and riddles, and my tales of people from my home district far away. It was on this investigative journey that we composed the 'Bird Verses' which every Tom, Dick and Harry now knows. We were of one mind during those sunny days and nights on the coast of Snjáfjöll. Láfi had begun the poem, the first three stanzas were his, but had run out of birds and inspiration by the time I turned up. As we walked from farm to farm we took to chanting the poem together. He recited the first verses, which he had knocked together with some skill, and I slid into the metre – slipped into it like a tongue into the eye socket of a well-boiled sheep's head. We composed like fury, casting one bird after another into the air before slotting it into place in our list. The light summer days and nights merged into one and, free from any timetable, we took no rest when the muse was upon us but allowed it to seize us and lift us to that higher plane of the poet's art that is sometimes called poetic ecstasy and resembles nothing so much as delirious happiness, for those under its influence tend to move with quick jerks of the limbs, rocked by gales of laughter and prone to madcap fits, such as rushing off, yelling words into the blue, one to the west, another to the east, the third up in the air, the fourth behind one, the fifth in front and the sixth at the ground, before plumping down on top of it, as if to crush any devil that might pop up its head at the unexpected message, and sit tight, rocking to and fro, babbling gibberish as one juggled the six words together until they formed a clever, well-crafted line. And so on until we nodded off with a half-made line of verse on our lips and slept where we fell, often till well past midday. Unfortunately, though, it was not always so, and most of the verses came into being like any other discussion between learned men. I even slipped in several alien bird species that Láfi had never heard of, like the noble pelican which builds a nest for its young in its beak and gives birth to them from the blood of its breast, or that Babel bird the parrot that speaks every tongue on Earth. When he cast doubt on the existence of such freaks, I answered his objections by saying:

'Who's to say that they haven't been blown here by the wind some time, cast ashore by gales or in the baggage of one of those foreign ships' captains who are forever turning up in Iceland with all kinds of odd cargo? Really, do you think anyone who ran into us in our madness would find it any stranger to hear of a sky-blue bird with red wings prating in Latin than to learn that men such as ourselves thrive in this land?'

'Well ...', Láfi replied, 'surely there's no such thing as the ostrich; one minute a flightless giant, the next a kind of bush?'

In the end the final verse came together just as we reached the part of the coast where the ghost was wreaking the greatest havoc. I doubt my tongue would have been as agile as it proved when our paths crossed, the living Jónas the Learned and the dead Phantom Jónsson, had I not oiled it with the Bird Verses during the previous week.

—

Where was it that we first encountered the boy? Ah yes, we were asleep in a grassy dell beneath a black crag, known as the Hafsteinn or Sea Rock, and I would sooner have expected a mysterious visitor from its bowels than the one who emerged from his cold grave to harass us. We were lying comatose after one of our poetic fits when I was roused by a movement in the scree above us to the east, as if little stones had been dislodged by a foot and rolled down the gravel bank with a dry rattle. Assuming it was a fox on the prowl, I closed my eyes and lay without moving, waiting for the animal to complete its journey across the scree. But when there were no further noises, I thought it wiser to take a look at this traveller. Holding my breath, I strained my ears. For a long moment there was no sound but the piping of the newly wakened oyster-catcher, strutting along the beach of the cove below us. Then I heard something tread warily into the thick moss on the other side of the rock. I realised at once that it must be the ghost come to meet us since no mortal creature could descend in a single stride from the scree to the heathery slope where Láfi and I were lying. I imagined it standing with one foot on high, the other down in the moss beside the rock, legs akimbo like a wishbone. I waited and the thing waited. I breathed out cautiously, without making a sound. There was a crack as the ghost's upper leg whipped down and smacked into its lower leg. Clacking knees like that would have been painful for a living man but the dead one uttered not so much as a whimper. Láfi was woken by the crack. He raised his head from the ground, about to start his sleep-drugged 'wha-wha-wha?' when I signalled to him to be quiet. He obeyed, turning his head towards me so that I could give him further indication as to what was afoot. As imperceptibly as we could, and with utmost slowness, we now turned our heads towards the corner of the rock in whose lee the demon was standing. I thought I saw a shadowy human shape moving there; evidently the ghost was waiting and watching us too.

Now the patience of the players was tested. The dead generally possess more fortitude than the living, as is clear by the way they lie still in their graves while man scurries around like a frightened field mouse, trembling and quivering in the rare moments that he pauses, resembling a mouse in that as well, but this time a house mouse that has fled from a cat into a crack in the wall and is listening for its footsteps, hoping that it will give up and leave, but unsure whether the cat is there or has gone, because a feline can also stand motionless for long periods without its knee-joints stiffening up. Láfi and I could expect Reverend Jón's dead son to vanquish us in any battle that is won by the player who waits longest. I heard Láfi sigh and saw his eyes darting around in his head, from the rock to the sky, while I disciplined myself to wait for what was to come. And it came, a horrible sight that hung in the air for a split second, like the face of the fellow who shares one's quarters, which floats before one's eyes in the darkness like a purple mask after the candle has been blown out: one, two, three and it is gone. So the apparition's loathsome head appeared and disappeared again as it craned it round the rock wall and scowled into my face. White skin, with a fist-sized bruise from the temple to the right-hand corner of its mouth, mouldering cheeks, hair straggling claw-like over its forehead above rolling, red, bestial eyes. The evil youth opened wide his skate's jaw, inside which all the teeth were broken at the root or smashed in from the fall that had sent him to his death on the slab of rock; he clicked his tongue loudly and vanished the instant Láfi looked his way. Láfi turned to me and started gasping and whining with fright, for the vision had left behind an expression of such terror on my face that it was more than enough to unman him. I understood now why he had been unable to tackle the task alone. But before I could pursue this thought any further, and before Láfi had finished his wailing, the ghost launched its attack. The parson's dead son sprang on to the crag, squatted on the edge and loosed the back flap of its breeches. Before we could dodge, it released a torrent of almost every imaginable kind of human filth: the excrement of men and livestock, human faeces and horse manure, lamb droppings, rotten eggs and animal bones, maggoty bird skins, the squitters of babes and fish guts, dead men's rags and all kinds of other muck. Under this deluge we scrambled to our feet, flinging out our arms to ward off the seemingly endless diabolical flood that continued for a good while even after we had fled on to the moor. My reading glass was buried under this colossal dung heap but I could not bring myself to dig it out of the filth, nor could Láfi be persuaded to do it for me. Many years would pass before I found another lens as handy, and you can imagine how this hindered me in my philosophical studies. From up on the crag the ghoul let out a rending screech as it finished. Shall we concur that the sun shone from a cloudless sky as we were drenched in the hideous downpour, and the moors smelt as sweet as moors can do on the loveliest summer's day? Well, I myself now reeked like the belch from a dead man's gullet. Stripping off by the nearest stream, we rinsed the ordure off ourselves and our clothes, and while they were drying we ate some breakfast and discussed what to do. The ghost was clearly ungovernable, bound neither by the rules of men nor those of higher powers; it had not only been banished from the realm of the living but also from that of the dead. We had to make it clear to the ghost where it belonged, now that it was deceased.

'It seems to me that the best way to go about it would be by the sort of exorcism that good priests used to perform in papist times, that is, to tell the ghoul the history of the world, of spirits and men, both evil and benevolent. In that way it will eventually see where it fits into God's great mechanism and realise that it is in quite the wrong place. For how is a dead man to tell the difference between himself and the living if he is still able to walk around, participate in fights and run errands? For that matter, how is he to know that he is not one of the elves? Both live outside human society. How is he to know that he is not a piece of driftwood? The flesh of both is equally rotten and stinking. Or a stray dog? Both are shooed away. Or merely a rock that rolls down the mountainside, causing men to dodge?' I said, and persisted doggedly:

'No, we must find this walking corpse a suitable resting place, we must find it the right shelf in the world's museum of curiosities, we must place it beside its peers, so that both it and any passer-by may see what kind it is, and thus both we and the ghost will be free of all fear and suffering. For when a thing has been classified correctly, it is tamed.'

Yes, Láfi and I would impress upon the corpse of the parson's son the workings of the world and its own place within it, after which it would hopefully find its way to the right door, in this case the coffin lid. But for this to work, I would have to browbeat it. Láfi glanced out of the corner of his eye and nodded, signalling that the ghost was sneaking up behind me. I spun round. Yes, there it stood, mouldering and hideous. I began the browbeating:

Christ's death upon the holy cross
has brought mankind salvation.
Twixt thee and me this fact I toss,
thou creature of damnation ...

And still I intoned:

All day we've knocked this fiend about
and harried him with our verse;
may it strike his jaw like a bloody great clout
and put an end to this curse.

At this, the apparition's lower jaw snapped against the upper with such force that its front teeth cracked to the root. Not that it could have answered me anyway as its tongue was too rotten to do more than growl and spit. And now it could not even do that, though its throat still rattled and the groans found their way out through its nose as it flinched under the verses, which became ever harder for it to bear the more skilfully and aptly they were composed. While I chanted, Láfi made sure that the ghost remained within earshot, for of course it fled from the message like a dog from curses, and was uncomfortably quick on its feet due to the length of its stride, as mentioned before. The corpse fled, not pausing in its flight except to stoop for stones or dirt or sheep droppings still warm from the rectum, which it flung at my head as I tore in pursuit, chanting as loudly as my lack of breath would allow, while Láfi ran alongside, trying to head it off or guide it towards rough terrain that would slow it down. Eventually, we managed to drive it into a marsh, where it sank up to its navel in a bog. I was now able to summon up before its mouldering eyes a picture of the horde of demons that fell to Earth when Lucifer was cast down from Heaven. Their multitude is like glowing motes in a sunbeam (they are swarming evil in search of something to stick to) or as many as the raindrops that fall in a downpour that lasts for nine days without stopping. Then I consoled it by explaining that it did not belong to that group. I described for it how the heavens rise and fall in relation to the moon, three in a row above and three in a row below. In these heavens dwell the ethereal spirits, endowed with various natures, some fine, some foul, though it is always perilous for people to swallow them and therefore not to be attempted except by well-equipped experts like Láfi and me. Under this onslaught the animate corpse struggled like a wolf in a trap, scrabbling in the spongy moss and trying in vain to heave itself out of the bog. I continued, turning now to its own case, telling it that revenants were the bodies of the dead who in life had been guilty of swearing at others; that on the corpses of such cursing wretches the doors stood wide open for the Devil himself to crawl inside. Which he did willingly, appointing himself the driver of the body and riding the deceased like a cruel jockey driving on his horse, except that in this case the vengeful heart formed the saddle in which the accursed rider sat as he drove his spurs into the rotten lungs. Once I had exposed the Prince of Darkness who was abusing the corpse of the parson's son, it was as if all the wind left its sails. Its body slumped, its arms fell to its sides and it hung forwards, trapped by the bog, like a drunken rider fallen asleep in the saddle, its matted hair swinging in the evening breeze. In this position it began to stiffen up, like the corpse it should by rights have been. A deathly silence fell on the countryside, the breeze caressed my cheek and I believed the Devil's corpse-ride was at an end. And so it was for a long moment. Then the corpse's mouth fell open and from where I was standing I noticed that a small butterwort growing on a nearby tussock imitated its movement; its flower-head opened with a quiet pop, releasing a midge that it had snapped up the instant the world fell silent. The fly had not been lying in the plant's digestive juices too long to prevent it from launching into flight, and with an ugly thunderous drone it flew straight into the dead man's mouth. Instantly all rigidity left the corpse as the Devil re-entered it in the form of this midge. The corpse tore itself out of the bog with a terrible howl and took flight, heading for the mountain with us close on its heels. But its strength was so depleted by its enforced sojourn under my fiend-scaring verses that Láfi caught up with it before it could squeeze all the way into a fissure in the rocks. Clutching its shanks, Láfi hauled with all his might against the ghost which was halfway down the cleft, hanging on grimly to a root or whatever it could grab. The wretched fiend was evidently trying to reach the place where it was happiest; in other words, Hell. At this I began my hectoring anew, commanding it to release the soul of the parson's son for judgement by God in Heaven, for only then would it be free to travel down the fifteen levels that separate the world of men from the inferno of Hell. At that it ceased all its struggling and our work was done. We dragged the corpse out of the hole and wiped the filth from its face, for although it was all battered and maggoty as described before, it now had the peaceful air of one who is well and truly dead. We carried the boy between us home to the parsonage, where the parson and his wife thanked us with kisses and cries of gratitude for laying the fiend that had forcibly taken up its abode in their son's body. Láfi and I received our appointed wages, which were not much to speak of once we had divided them up between us but more than enough when one considers the fame we acquired by this deed. We did not dine at the farm, having had our fill of the stinking corpse, but took the food we were given and hurried up the mountain with our tent. It was the longest day of the year, my last night with Láfi, and the prospects were good for poetry. The following day I would head south to Sigga and Pálmi Gudmundur, our firstborn. I was full of grand plans, mindful of the fame that the destruction of a malevolent ghost was bound to bring me, the anticipated renown that would elevate me to the giddy heights of esteem, from which vantage point I would be able to survey the world as my playground. Just as I was thinking this thought, I was startled by a gruff voice saying:

'Make the most of your fame!'

It is my poor old lady, Sigrídur. Instead of answering, I merely pat the tussock at my side and so the two of us sit, watching the sun complete its circuit of the Earth. It climbs aslant up the cloud-foamy sea of sky, sailing in a fine arc to the horizon where it perches for an instant like a dandelion seed which just touches a wet stone before the wind lifts it away.

Kidney Stone

Dazzling light: when the day is such a brilliant blue-white that the firmament is no longer a frame for the burning sun, rather the sun has become the kindling for a brilliant silver curtain that rises at the horizon and is drawn across the entire visible world, while the mountain ranges to the north, west and south shimmer as if in a mirage, sometimes in shadow, sometimes in sunlight, but never still; and the sea is a sheet of billowing velvet, stretching from the shores of the island to the hem of the sky, while the island itself, glittering in its midst, is a yellow-gold button on a downy cushion, waiting to be dented by the head of the heavenly child; and the whole vision is run through with tinkling bright silk thread, nimbly tacked between earth and sea and sky and fiery sun with the great needle that can pierce every element. But tracing the blazing needlework means little to the human eye, for although one line springs from another, like vein branching from vein on a birch leaf or the back of one's hand or a precious stone, this magnificent play of light is so small when set against eternity that to perceive the whole picture the spectator would have to step back into the next world, to stand beside the throne of the One who in the beginning opened His mouth and uttered the words: 'Let there be light!'

And there was dazzling light.

Jónas the Learned sits on a rock by the shore, gazing at this world which has silently merged into a single point of light. He has not taken his eyes off it since he sat down and the vision first began to take form, and now his pupils are like grains of sand, the protective film of tears has dried up; he urgently needs to blink but cannot lest the vision disappear before he can fix its details in his memory, which is essential if he is to interpret it. But in the end there is no avoiding it, either he must draw down the lids over his eyes or else he will go blind. He blinks. But instead of dissolving, the vision gains an addition: far to the north-west, in the angle of a cove where land meets sea in a glimmering mirage, a tiny black spot appears and begins slowly to move out into the bay. Careful not to lose sight of the sailing dot, Jónas shifts on his hard stone seat and takes a deep breath: this could be a long wait. He opens his eyes wide and keeps them like that until an infernal cramp seizes every muscle in his head, from the corners of his mouth to his crown, and his face is distorted into a ludicrous mask of suffering, but by then the dot has grown to the size of the smallest fingernail on an infant's hand and the spectator dares to close his lids again for an instant. Next time Jónas looks at the dot it has changed shape and is no longer a dot but a diamond, a black diamond sliding over the silky smooth sea: it is the prow of a boat and that boat is making for the island.

There is a man standing in the bow – the watcher on shore squints in the hope of recognising him (could they be bringing him supplies?), but the light falls on the man's back – as yet he is only the silhouette of a man – and he raises his right hand in a grand gesture, as if waving to Jónas Pálmason the Learned. Jónas is about to wave back but lets his hand fall in his lap when he sees that the greeting was assuredly not intended for him. For as soon as the man's arm comes to a stop above his head there is such a whooshing of feathers that the wind blows from all directions at once as every last bird in the north obeys the man's command, swiftly swooping in from land and sea. Whether they have been endowed with large wings or small, speckled coats or black stockings, whether they are short of beak or long of shank, with heather in their crop or sand eels in their gullet, the birds answer the summons and circle like a whirlwind over the man, calling, squawking, chirping, until each finds its place in the sky above his head. When the down finally ceases to snow from their wings, Jónas sees that the flock has formed a living fan over the boat, in which a pair of each species (cock and hen, drake and duck, gander and goose) has lined up according to size, from the wren, fluttering at shoulder height around the man in the bow, to the puffin which flaps frantically somewhat higher, to the piping whimbrel hovering above the mallard but below the cruel eagle, right up to the swans, cob and pen, beating wings so white that they rival the silvery firmament.

After studying this vision for a while, Jónas blinked, at which the man lowered his arm and pointed to the surface of the sea. In an instant the sea became as clear as a cool autumn evening and the boat appeared to be hanging in thin air rather than floating on water, for the ocean had grown so translucent that its bed could be seen far and wide, even to the horizon. Jónas saw now that the island was like a tapering peak; he sat not on a rock on the beach but on the edge of a precipice. Then the glassy sea began to boil, the deeps churned and now the fish came swimming with rapid flaps of their tails, from south and east, from the shallows by the shore and the trenches beyond. There were redfish and whiting, shark and plaice, sea scorpion and halibut, thorny skate and cod, herring and seal, and all the other fish Jónas the Learned knew and others he did not. Observing the same rule as the birds in the sky, they arranged themselves according to size, from the keel of the boat to the bottom of the sea, sticklebacks at the top, sperm whales at the bottom, and so many species in between that when each pair was in place the shoal spread out in the clear brine like a scallop shell, a glittering reflection of the flying fan above. There was no respite for Jónas's eyes as he cast his gaze hither and thither between sky and sea, memorising the appearance of the birds and fishes, their similarities in colour and shape, redwing and redfish ...

All the while this spectacle lasted, the boat slid ever closer to the island – moving of its own accord though there was no wind in that still, cloudless, dazzling world – and had Jónas paid any attention to the figure standing in the bow he would have seen that he was a man in his forties, clad in a coat of grey-brown or grey-speckled homespun, with a homespun hat of the same colour on his head, while under the brim could be glimpsed eyes that seemed to glow like glass orbs. The man swung his arm again, drawing the naturalist's attention from the creatures of the heights and depths: this time he pointed to land. Then it appeared to Jónas as if in a revelation that from the shores of the sea to the peaks of the glacier a specimen of every kind of plant nourished by Icelandic soil tore itself willingly from mould and gravel – everything from the forget-me-not to the rowan tree – and the flowers of earth rose into the sky, light as mist from a mountain tarn. High in the sky, the grasses and herbs classed themselves according to their growth, twining together to form a vast garland that danced over the barren wastes, giving off a perfume so sweet that Jónas nearly swooned. But he had to stay awake for the spectacle was not over: now the land animals entered the stage on a mossy stone, the fox and the field mouse; the little mice perching serenely between the foxes' ears.

The man in the boat repeated his last movement, drawing back his outstretched arm and swinging it to shore. The ground opened. The mountains soughed off their screes so that one could see deep into their bowels, where countless metals, crystals and precious stones lay on different ledges, sparkling and glittering, many ancient, others newborn, reddened by the glow of subterranean fires and bathed in the waters of underground rivers.

'Yes, yes … Oh yes!'

Jónas Pálmason the Learned rocked on his boulder. Yes, there it was on the topmost seat, the highest ledge of all – that dearly bought metal that he had always suspected lay concealed in the unkind flesh of his motherland, the very blood of the earth: gold!

'Did I not say so? They …'

He got no further. There was a blare of trumpets.

'Hoo-hoo-hoo!'

It is the swans, thrumming their vocal cords. The other creatures fall silent, the sea trout gently flicking its tail, the raven softly flapping its wings. The feathery trumpets sound a second time. Jónas looks up and realises that the boat is nearing land. He rises to go and meet the boatman, buttoning up his jacket, running a hand through his hair. But then he becomes aware that the fanfare was not intended to welcome the boat. Far out on the rim of the sea to the north appears a school of whales which swim rapidly south across the bay.

'Hoo-hoo …'

The clarion call is to welcome these newcomers

to the game. In a synchronised water dance they dive beneath the boat and shoot their heads out of the sea beyond: twelve narwhals from Greenland. They raise their twisted horns, seven ells long, to the sky, clash them together and cross them like the lances of a guard of honour, the whole dance conducted to the sound of high-pitched singing and a great splashing of fins. With this the vision is complete, an intricate, carefully thought-out coat of arms:

Bird in air,
mammal on moor,
fish in sea,
plant on shore.
Stone in ground,
man in the middle,
monsters of the sound,
submissive – no more?

—

The dazzling light played on the retinas of Jónas Pálmason the Learned, who had seen nothing so fair in all his sixty-three years on Earth. Ever since he reached manhood he had secretly longed for the good Lord to reveal to him the order of things, to allow him to examine how the world mechanism is put together. Once, when he and Sigrídur lived at Uppsandar, he thought he perceived in the sky the outlines of a colossal foot that rested on the globe of the Earth. The sole was contiguous with the surface of the sea and the heel rested on the lowland beneath the glacier, while the shape of the ankle could just be made out where the sun stood at its noontide zenith. It must have been an angel.

Jónas fell to his knees, tears welling up in his eyes, his tongue dry and cleaving to the roof of his mouth. He lay down on his side, knees drawn up under his chin; he had gooseflesh, a headache and cramps in his muscles and guts. He broke out in a cold sweat. His senses had been strained beyond what a human can bear.

'Oh, do not let me lose my mind! I must hold on to my wits so that I can fix this revelation in a poem ...'

He heard a crunch in the sand. A booted foot was planted beside his head. Jónas looked up: the man was standing over him. His boat was resting in a bed of seaweed. Nothing else of the vision remained. Man and boat, that was all. Sky and sea had recovered their true form. From Jónas's point of view, the man was framed by clouds which darkened the lower one looked. A gull mewed. It was going to rain.

The stranger held out his hand to Jónas. It was an elegant, spatulate hand, the middle finger of which sported a silver ring engraved with an inscription. Jónas accepted the proffered hand and the man raised him to his feet. Still without releasing Jónas's hand, he studied him curiously and said:

'Good day to you, Jón Gudmundsson the Learned.'

Jónas did not return his look. He was so preoccupied with trying to read the inscription on the ring that he apparently failed to notice that the man had addressed him by the wrong name. He returned the greeting absent-mindedly:

'Yes, good day yourself ...'

Before Jónas could make out a single word of the inscription, the man let go of his hand and, turning away from Jónas, said with authority:

'I've come to fetch you. You're to prepare yourself for a journey.'

Jónas stopped brushing the sand off his clothes. Had he heard right? Was he free? The man continued:

'You're to bring with you your drawing lead and wood-carving knife, which will come in useful where you'll be spending the winter.'

'And where is that?'

'You're going to Copenhagen ...'

Jónas's heart took a leap and he bounced on the spot, then raced off towards the hut, calling:

'Sigrídur, we're leaving! We're free!'

But Sigrídur Thórólfsdóttir was not there. Jónas scanned his surroundings. He bounded up the slope above the hut, which gave a view of the whole island. Sigrídur was nowhere to be seen. He called her name, again and again. The man was bending over his boat on the beach, paying Jónas no heed. Jónas ran to him and clutched at his coat, squawking repeatedly:

'Where is she, what have you done with her?'

The man did not answer. Nor did he look up from his task. Moving without haste he placed one oar in a cleft amidships where it stood firm like a mast. This seemed such a curious arrangement to Jónas that it rendered him momentarily silent, giving the man a chance to speak:

'Just do as I told you and fetch your gear.'

'But what about Sigrídur?'

The stranger turned and Jónas saw his face for the first time. He backed away. The man had rather a small head with a face that narrowed towards the chin, a moustache and beard, and whiskers growing to the middle of his cheeks. Before his eyes he wore two glass lenses which sat in a frame which was fixed behind his ears. As Jónas leant forward to examine this contrivance more closely, the man shot out his left hand, caught hold of Jónas's shirt and pulled the island-dweller close. Laying his mouth to his ear, he said quietly:

'Sigrídur is standing in the hut doorway. You're still caught up in your vision; that's why you can't see her.'

Jónas looked round and saw out of the corner of his eye that it was true. There was nobody standing in the doorway of the hut. He lost his footing, the cramp twisted his guts again and he felt faint. He wanted to lie down, to curl up on the sand. The man tightened his grip on his shirt, held Jónas upright and whispered:

'We'll make sure she's still here when you return ...'

With his right hand he opened the neck of Jónas's shirt and, splaying his fingers, ran his manicured nails quick as a flash along the rib in Jónas's right side – the fifth, whether one is counting from top or bottom – flaying skin and flesh to the bone, right round to the back where he snapped the rib from the spine, then jerked it vigorously until the front end broke off the cartilage that connected it to the breastbone. Jónas felt no pain in spite of the blood that gushed from the wound and ran along the man's fingers and down the back of his hand to his wrist. The man brandished the bone under his nose. The rib was fattier than Jónas would have expected: the summer had been kind to him and Sigrídur. He had managed to lure away a nine-week-old seal pup from the colony that bred on the southern side of the island. It had made a good feast. In fact, they had eaten more of it than they meant to and cured less for the winter. Jónas was delighted to see how much of the seal fat had transferred itself from the pup to him.

The man flung the rib-bone away:

'That's where you'll find her!'

The bone landed in the doorway of the hut and bounced from there into a bed of heather beside the path below, where it came to a standstill. The man released his grip on Jónas and, pulling out a white handkerchief, began to wipe the blood from his hand:

'Hurry up now ...'

Jónas found his footing on the shingle and fumbled at the wound which had already healed, leaving nothing behind but a pink scar and a hollow where the rib had been. Having tied up his shirt points, he hurried to the hut. He stuffed stockings, undershirt, knee breeches, a woollen jersey, hood and mittens into his haversack. Writing instruments, whittling knives, blank pages, a small dice-shaped box of seal-bone and a pocket-sized book went into his satchel. This was all he had for the long journey ahead. He donned his leather hat. The man was standing beside the boat, ready to assist his passenger aboard. Jónas trod the path down to the beach. When he came to where the bone was lying in the heather he could not contain himself. Flinging himself on all fours he pressed hot, tear-soaked kisses on his rib:

'Good and best of wives, my darling mistress, mother of my children, Sigrídur Thórólfsdóttir, may God bless you and protect you in your solitude, in the condition, unnatural to any woman, of living without male guidance ... May He keep you and answer your prayers in your widowed state if pirates should take me as their prize ... May He strengthen you in your anguish if you learn that I have been forced into servitude through the action of my enemies ... May He comfort you if I am stabbed to death by brigands ... May He wrap you in His great, merciful embrace should an evil sea serpent wind itself around my vessel and smash it to pieces, killing everyone on board and me as well ... May He take pity on us and allow us to meet again in the wide halls of Heaven if, disgusted by mankind's evil deeds, He decides to destroy His creation while we are still separated by land and sea, while you are here and I am there ... May His fatherly countenance watch over you ...'

It grew suddenly dark and drizzle began to fall from the sky. The man ran to Jónas, raised him to his feet and, putting an arm round his shoulders, supported him down to the water's edge where he helped him on board the boat, settled him amidships and made him hold on to the oar that stood upright there like a mast. With the other oar he pushed off from the landing place. The keel grated on the bottom, the oar-blade creaked. Finally the boat was free, rocking gently on the swell. Pulling in the oar, the man placed it parallel to the keel and took a seat on the stern thwart.

The vessel made a south-easterly course into the swiftly falling dusk. They sailed without speaking. After a little while it occurred to Jónas that the wound in the Saviour's side had been in the same place as that which was formed when Adam's rib was removed. He was about to open a conversation on the subject but stopped when he saw that the man was nodding off in his seat. They could discuss it later. The dusk deepened. Jónas looked around and noticed that there was a little pennant bound to the top of the oar: a red wing on a white background. It was the handkerchief stained with Jónas's blood, bearing the man's handprint.

The darkness was almost complete when the man stirred and pointed with the toe of his right boot to a long, tapering box which was lashed down firmly in the bow. It emitted a disagreeable rattling croak. He said:

'That's for Ole Worm ...'

At that the darkness turned pitch black, so black that it can only be compared to the dazzling whiteness that reigned at the outset of Jónas's vision.

—

In early September 1636 Jónas Pálmason the Learned was fetched from Gullbjörn's Island and conveyed in secret to the south of Iceland. After five days' riding he was brought to the trading post of Bakki on the south coast and that same evening put on board a merchant ship which was due to sail on the morning tide. He did not know who was behind his transportation but their treatment of him was gentler than what he had been accustomed to from men in authority, and conditions on board were better than a convict could hope for; instead of being confined in the prison hold he was allowed to sleep with the crew. The whole undertaking was a mystery to him. Back when his trial for the book of sorcery that he had allegedly compiled, and the school of necromancy that he had allegedly run, had resulted in the severest sentence of outlawry, with the proviso that no one was to shelter or assist him in any way, Jónas had tried in vain to leave the country. He had trekked with his wife and children from one end of Iceland to the other, to wherever a ship might put to shore, begging a passage, but no one would take them aboard. Whether this was from fear of carrying a sorcerer or from malice, or else a conspiracy by Jónas's enemies – who might be able to secure an even harsher penalty, perhaps even death, if he violated the terms of his exile – we shall never know, but this reluctance to allow him to comply with his sentence condemned him to outlawry in his own land for five long years, until without warning or explanation he was carried on board the ship which was now rocking him to sleep on the night swell in Bakki Harbour.

At first light, as the ship was weighing anchor, another passenger was brought on board. Jónas woke up when a man with a canvas sack over his head was led through the sleeping quarters by two guards in the employ of Prosmund, the Danish governor of Iceland. After ordering the prisoner to sit on the deck diagonally opposite Jónas's hammock, they removed his shackles and left. The new arrival moaned pitifully and winced as he fiddled with the knot that held the sack firmly in place on his head; his hands, blue from the irons, fumbled helplessly. Jónas rolled out of his hammock and loosed the sack from the man's head. From beneath the canvas emerged a face with a fair beard and mournful blue eyes. It was his son, Reverend Pálmi Gudmundur Jónasson. Father and son fell weeping and wailing into each other's arms, and wept together in the cabin for so long that a sailor eventually drove them up on deck, where they wept some more until they had almost wept away the terrifying but compelling sight of the land disappearing below the horizon.

Father and son sailed the seas and came safely to harbour.

In those first few hours after he stepped ashore in Copenhagen, Jónas the Learned saw more people than he had hitherto seen in the whole of his life: more aprons, more hats, more boots, more chickens, more pigs, more horses, more wheelbarrows, more dogs, more soldiers, more cannon, more wagons, more roofs, more buildings, more windows, more doors. And also many things he had only ever seen in pictures: windmills and water pumps, towers and market squares, churches and castles, sculptures and friezes, trees and ponds, cobblers and tailors, cheese merchants and muleteers. He tried not to let any of it impinge on his consciousness, tried to ignore all the new buildings, for he longed above all to be carried away by the illusion that he had arrived in the realm of Gormur the Old, the ancient king of the Danes. The feeling had first begun to grow in him when they sighted the Faroe Islands during the voyage. At last Jónas was seeing with his own eyes something he had drawn on those maps of the world that he had been able at times to use as payment for hospitality or provisions when he and Sigga were on the run with their children. But instead of poring over paper, looking down from heaven as if with the eye of the highest flying bird, he himself was on the map. And he was seized by the conviction that when he set foot on Danish soil all roads would be open to him. For Jónas had reached the place where the white background on maps ends – that expanse which the draughtsman feels compelled to decorate with monsters and seahorses and floating polar bears to prevent the eye from growing bored of the ocean – he had reached land in a place that was strangely familiar to him, although hitherto he had known it only as his own handiwork, realised in birch ink and paint; faint, of course, to keep the place names legible. Being accustomed to thinking of the world as a picture that can be folded up and put away in one's pocket, or a terse geographical treatise by a medieval historian, he had the impression that from where he was now it was but a short hop to all the main sites of history: south to Constantinople and the Holy Land, east to Sweden and Tartary, to Novaya Zemlya and Asia.

But the sights that met his eyes were nothing to the assaults on his ears, for everything had its own attendant noise: rattling, cackling, shouting, banging, barking, jingling, neighing, belching, cracking, grunting, whining, clapping, and the thunderous footsteps of man and beast, running, limping, ambling, tramping. To be sure, Jónas could limit his field of vision by walking close behind Reverend Pálmi Gudmundur, eyes fixed between his shoulder blades – which he did despite his son's constant complaints that he was treading on his heels – but he could not shut out the noise. He could not block his ears since both his hands were full. In one he was carrying a bundle of clothes belonging to their guide, a student from the south of Iceland who in return for help with his luggage was going to show them to a tolerable inn, while in the other he was holding the oblong box which reached from his fist down to his ankle. No, to have muffled the din of the city he would have had to pour wax in his ears.

Jónas Pálmason the Learned was one of those people whose life is forever turning with the wheel of fortune. He had no sooner reached a safe haven than he was sent straight back out on to the stormy sea, and always in a leakier vessel than the one in which he had arrived. Father and son took rooms at an inn called the Sommerfugl, or Butterfly, which Jónas nicknamed 'the Summer Snipe' after the harbinger of summer on his island; a respectable lodging for decent men and a sign that Providence was apparently prepared to handle him and Reverend Pálmi Gudmundur with silk gloves from now on.

Indeed, his stay at the inn was so delightful in comparison with his exile on the island or being tossed at sea on the merchant ship that for the first week he could not be persuaded to leave the house but lay all day long in bed, haltingly reading a recent edition of *Aesop's Fables*. Besides, he was fairly insulated there from the hubbub of the city. Reverend Pálmi Gudmundur on the other hand dashed all over town, working to resolve their case, which was the purpose of their journey after all: to obtain a royal writ dismissing the charges against them. He went hither and thither among those of their countrymen who he had reason to believe would be well disposed towards him and his father, asking their advice on how best to bring the matter to the attention of the king, for it would take no less than a handwritten, sealed writ from His Majesty King Christian IV to induce the judges of the Icelandic Althing to change their minds. And that was easier said than done. Reverend Pálmi Gudmundur discovered in addition that those responsible for their passage to Denmark were a group of scholars who had grown weary of Ole Worm's incessant questions about this Jónas the Learned, who the Danish professor was convinced possessed a vast fund of knowledge about the ancient runic alphabet. For six years they had given him the same answer: that little was known of this Jónas beyond the fact that he was continually on the run from the authorities, a condemned man who infected all who came near him with his misfortunes. In the end, however, when Dr Wormius had contrived it so that the University Council was prepared to take up Jónas's cause, and his son's too if need be, his Icelandic colleagues could no longer ignore the requests of their brother in academia and personal friend of the king, so they had instigated a whip-round to pay for Jónas's passage. And they sent Reverend Pálmi Gudmundur with him in the hope that the troublesome father and son would never return to Iceland.

By dint of telling Jónas that one of the stalls by the harbour had a monkey on display, Reverend Pálmi Gudmundur finally managed to rouse his father's interest in seeing more of Copenhagen than the inn and its garden. Ever since Jónas had read Aesop's fable about the monkey and the fox, he had been puzzling over the paradox that the animal which most resembled man should be bested by a four-footed beast with apparently human wits. He now longed to see a monkey with his own eyes, having seen more than enough of foxes. But before Jónas the Learned could abandon his straw mattress for the monkey, the machinery of Fate creaked into action once more; news came to the ears of father and son that their enemies from Iceland had reached Copenhagen before them and already launched a campaign of slander. The fiends had compiled a scroll containing all the vilest and most vicious things that had ever been said or written about Jónas the Learned, largely derived from the polemic by Reverend Gudmundur Einarsson of Stadarstadur, commonly known as the Treatise but described by himself as '*In versutias serpentis recti et tortuosi*, that is, a little treatise against the deceits and machinations of the Devil who works sometimes by straight, sometimes by crooked ways, to ruin the redemption of mankind.' The juiciest morsels of this stew were highly seasoned with warnings to the Danes not to take pity on a scoundrel like Jonas, let alone permit him entry to the country, or, perish the thought, risk sheltering scum like him in Copenhagen, where Mayor Juren had long been troubled by an obscure but agonising internal complaint for which he had undergone extortionately expensive and painful cures that had achieved little but to keep him hanging on at death's door. But since it was commonly rumoured that witchcraft lay at the root of his disease, no cost should be spared in tracking down the culprit. In such an atmosphere it proved easy for Jónas's enemies to sow the seeds of mistrust and ill will towards him. In consequence, one noontide in mid-October a group of constables stormed the inn and arrested Jónas in the name of the king.

He was dragged before a magistrate at the City Hall where the slanderous scroll against him was read aloud and given credence, despite its mediocre composition – it lacked both tail and hind legs – and Jónas was sentenced to be transported back to Iceland. However, as there would be no ships now until spring, he was to remain in custody until that time. The magistrate paid no heed to Jónas, or rather to Reverend Pálmi Gudmundur on his behalf – since Jónas could not speak a word for the lump in his throat – who explained that he had come to Copenhagen to pursue his rights over a miscarriage of justice that had been perpetrated at the Althing, and, quite apart from that, he was a special envoy with a gift for none other than Olaus Wormius and his errand had not yet been fulfilled. The learned professor would unquestionably confirm that Jónas was not the dangerous criminal described in the letter. Was the magistrate unaware that he was known as 'the Learned'? The magistrate did not listen, any more than he had listened to the other defences that Reverend Pálmi Gudmundur pleaded on behalf of his father. In the end, however, it was the gift for the esteemed Rector Ole Worm that decided the matter by lending support to the idea of Jónas's dubious character, for it was a live Great Auk.

The creature had already caused alarm among the other guests at the Sommerfugl Inn, being unlike any bird they had ever seen, not only larger and more imposing but with a hoarse voice and a croak like the death rattle of a choking man. For the first few days Jónas had taken the Great Auk down to the dining room with him, placing the oblong box at his side, removing the lid and feeding the bird herring, which was plentiful in this country. The creature liked the food as much as the Danes did, though Jónas himself retched at every mouthful of this fatty inedible muck. After dinner he had permission to air the bird in the back garden. There was no danger of its escaping when he let it out of its cage, since it could not fly and was easy to corner. It was the Great Auk's evening perambulations that had filled the onlookers with such misgivings; the manner in which the bird, if it was a bird, waddled about among the hens, upright like a mannikin, conjured up ghastly tales from the dark recesses of the mind: tales of people who had been lucky to escape alive from the clutches of witches on Walpurgisnacht, being left dumb, disfigured and a burden to themselves and their families for the rest of their lives, or rather the descriptions of the witches' corporeal familiars. These were often a mixture of man and beast, not unlike the oddity that stood alone in the hen coop, bathed in moonlight, like a miniature version of a long-nosed witch swathed in a black cloak. For the bird was alone; the hens were all in their house, huddled together trembling, showing an uncanny fear of the malignant-looking visitant. At least the innkeeper's testimony before the court went something along these lines when he was cross-examined about the conduct of the accused, Jónas Pálmason the Learned, during the fortnight he had stayed at the Sommerfugl Inn. No other witnesses were called; the Icelander was clapped in irons forthwith and transferred to a new and worse place, Gaoler Rasmussen's House of Correction. There he discovered for himself that Copenhagen is like Lady Luck: capricious to many, but especially to Jónas.

—

It is time to introduce a contemporary of Jónas Pálmason the Learned, a man who not only authored the natural history treatise, 'The account of an animal which falls from the clouds in Norway and rapidly devours the inhabitants' grass and corn to their great detriment ...', but also devoted more time to studying antiquities than any other scholar in the first half of the seventeenth century, earning himself the title of Father of Nordic Antiquarianism. He is perhaps the finest example of a seventeenth-century man of science: a polymath with an insatiable thirst for knowledge who studied most branches of human knowledge; indeed there was no area of learning in which he did not take an interest. Moreover, his work was of such importance for Icelandic literature, and he had such close dealings with Icelanders, that his name deserves to be celebrated. This man was the doctor and natural philosopher, Ole Worm.

After the University Council had announced its verdict in the case of Jónas Pálmason the Learned on Wednesday 15 April 1637, the newly acquitted troublemaker was fetched from his cell beneath the chamber in the Consistorium building and taken with all haste to the laboratory of Preceptor Worm, who had personally directed his trial. Jónas was thus given his freedom within the university's area of jurisdiction and spared the dungeon where he should by rights have languished until Christian IV had confirmed his acquittal. Upon arrival they took the Icelander directly to the laundry. There his shackles were removed, he was forcibly deloused and de-fleaed, and finally dumped in the large cauldron which was in the normal course of things used to boil the slime and feathers off the myriad exotic animal skeletons and bird skins that Dr Worm acquired for his collection from every corner of the world. After the bath, they found the servant in the rector's employment who most resembled Jónas in build, and this small pot-bellied person was ordered to lend the newcomer a complete suit of clean clothes. On returning home to his laboratories, the master of the house found his guest in the kitchen sitting alone over his food, though with a large audience as his stay in prison had done nothing to improve his manners. As a puerile prank they had continued to bring him dishes long after he had eaten his fill – amused at the sight of him stuffing his cheeks – for Jónas, who knew no moderation after months of incarceration, fell ravenously upon everything that was laid before him. It was evident to Worm that he would burst if things carried on this way. And so the first encounter between the self-taught Jónas Pálmason and the academic Ole Worm was rather more intimate than the latter had intended. He ordered the suffering man to be taken to the very clinic in which he examined and cured the leading members of Copenhagen society, and when it became apparent that the patient's banquet would not budge, the doctor administered both emetic and enema. As a result of these vigorous purges, the rotund servant was required to lend Jónas a second suit of clothes, and with the renewed onset of Jónas's hunger pangs he was brought more food, though this time the meal was conducted under the watchful eye of the physician.

Early next morning Jónas the Learned was summoned to Ole Worm's study, where he discovered that it was not from benevolence alone that he had been spared a longer sojourn in the Blue Tower. He had no sooner taken a seat facing his benefactor than the latter began to grill him on the most unrelated of topics, though principally on runes and other heathen lore in the sagas of the ancient Icelanders: 'Tell me about the mound dwellers' script', 'Who was Bragi?', 'What does *futhark* mean?' Jónas grew nervous and feigned ignorance, pretending not to understand the questions even when Worm spoke in Danish, or else answered at random 'oh' and 'er', and sometimes 'well'. This shilly-shallying lasted until noon, when a man was sent out to fetch Reverend Pálmi Gudmundur, who explained to his father that Worm's interest in the heathen past was purely scholarly and that nothing he spoke of within the university walls would be used against him. Jónas was not entirely convinced. But Reverend Pálmi Gudmundur had also brought along Jónas's belongings: his paints, knives, books and papers – and the Great Auk that he had been feeding over the winter. The collector was delighted to receive a living specimen of this fabled avian oddity and embraced the giver, kissing him repeatedly. Worm apologised to Jónas for having overwhelmed him with questions for which he was unprepared, but he had been so excited to meet the learned Icelander in the flesh that he could not contain himself. He showed Jónas the replies he had received to the numerous letters he had written to his countrymen enquiring after him, and Reverend Pálmi Gudmundur translated them from Latin for the benefit of their subject. Magnús of Laufás, for instance, had written: 'From what I have heard, you will shortly receive a visit from the man who is the finest runic scholar among us despite the heavy sentence he has been given for sorcery – he will be travelling on Commissioner Rosenkrantz's ship, I gather. With him at your side you will have verbal answers to the points that seem unclear in the interpretation and if you wish you can with his help "seek gold from the dung-heap of Ennius". His name is Jónas Pálmason, called "the Learned", and from what I have been told he is knowledgeable on many subjects.' Jónas was standing on tiptoe by the end of the reading. The upshot was that he agreed to remain in lodging with Dr Worm, while Reverend Pálmi Gudmundur returned to prepare his defence for the imminent hearing of his own appeal.

The days now passed in discourse of runes and old Icelandic poetry. Ole Worm placed many riddles before Jónas on the Eddic and Skaldic compilations of Snorri Sturluson, which he was able to answer straight off. The previous year Worm had published a history of the runic art entitled *Danica literatura antiquissima, vulgo Gothica dicta*, and he now received confirmation of his suspicions that it contained much that was mistaken or obscure. But the university rector had other duties to attend to besides tapping Jónas's wisdom, and this gave the latter the chance to observe the work in Worm's collection of natural history and curiosities, known as the Museum Wormianum. Here the collector had assembled a vast array of organic specimens and objects related to his many fields of study: medicine, antiquarianism, philosophy, the natural history of animals, minerals and plants, and also works of art and antiquities. An elite team of the rector's favourite students was busy cataloguing the collection, arranging the objects on shelves and in drawers, hanging them on walls or from ceiling beams, or displaying them on specially built plinths. Here Jónas set eyes for the first time on many marvels that he had hitherto only read about in books: there were large pieces of coral, ostrich eggs, lemming skins and petrified dragons' teeth – for the collection was not only the largest of its kind in the world but unusual for being founded on the strictest scientific principles rather than the magpie fascination for glittering objects and childish glee in hoarding that tended to characterise the collections of electors and queens. Ole Worm was preparing to publish a catalogue of the museum's curiosities, and the students were engaged in recording the names and provenance of the objects according to the curator's careful system, as well as finding engravings of them in older scientific writings or else sketching pictures of those that had never before appeared in print. Not all the young men were equally skilled draughtsmen and as a result the illustration of the work was progressing more slowly than it should, until one of the students came upon Jónas the Learned sitting alone in the library with his paints, beguiling the time by copying the illustration of the bearded lady in a dress from Aldrovandi's *Monstrorum historia*, which he naturally executed with consummate skill. He was enlisted forthwith to sketch the objects in pencil for others to finish in ink. Worm praised his museum team for their increased productivity and the quality of the drawings, and Jónas got to indulge in his favourite pastime while at the same time examining Worm's objects and books. And so things continued until the time came to catalogue an object that was kept in a locked cabinet in the natural philosopher's study. This precious item was borne into the museum with great ceremony, and two lancers from the royal bodyguard no less were set to guard the door. The object was about five ells long, wrapped in a cloth of scarlet velvet with the insignia of Christian IV embroidered on it in gold, and naturally the learned doctor saw personally to its handling and cataloguing, for he had been graciously permitted to borrow it for purposes of research from the king's private collection. The students crowded around the long examination table to watch as Worm ran his gloved hands over the cloth, deftly drawing it back to reveal a magnificent unicorn's horn. But this was no ordinary specimen of the shy beast's cranial ornament, for the horn was fixed in a fragment of skull-bone. The spectators gasped: it was most unusual for any remains to be found of a unicorn besides the splendid twisted horn; other bones were extremely rare and scholars were more or less agreed that those found in museums were fake. But here was part of the forehead and crown of the beast, which could therefore be compared to the head of other cloven-hoofed creatures, for the unicorn was generally regarded as being most closely related to the ibex.

Jónas Pálmason the Learned began to laugh and could not stop. His short legs buckled under his quaking body and he dropped to the floor, where he lay hooting as if he were in tears. The students exchanged glances; they were ready for anything with Jónas, who was always mumbling to himself and blurting out non sequiturs, but this wild behaviour was both sinister and inappropriate in the presence of the rector and the royal treasure.

The lifeguards, who had not encountered Jónas before but considered themselves as adept as university men at identifying lunatics, grew uneasy and tightened their grip on their lances. Everyone waited in suspense for the reaction of the learned and courteous yet severe Preceptor Worm. Leaving the table, he took up position beside the laughing man, inclined his head and frowned, holding his beard and stroking it down over his chest, as if confronted with an unusual form of malady.

After long reflection, the learned doctor straightened up and exclaimed:

'Well, I might have known it ...'

And he too was seized with uncontrollable laughter. Bending down, he extended a hand and helped Jónas to his feet, declaring between fits of mirth:

'Of course, of course!'

Still chuckling, he ordered his assistants to wrap up the unicorn's horn and return it to his study. When this had been done, Worm and Jónas retired there themselves, laughing together. The students mimicked their master: 'Of course, of course!', though ignorant, naturally, of what had prompted his exclamation. Of one thing they could be sure: their master's roars of laughter were a sign that he had made a remarkable discovery. Worm was such an inveterate scholar that he was never more amused than when he discovered that he had been wrong.

—

It would perhaps be putting it too strongly to say that Rector Ole Worm, Doctor Medicinæ in Academia Hafniensi Professor Regius, had been wrong about the existence of the unicorn. In fact, he had for some time been assailed by doubts about the origin and nature of these marvellous horns. He had begun to wonder why so few people had actually set eyes on the beast in modern times; the most recent eyewitness accounts were all over a hundred years old, and there was moreover the conundrum of why nothing was ever found of their bodies apart from the horn. No one doubted the unicorn's noble nature; it was the touchstone of piety and chastity, as was proved by the fact that only young virgins could tame its savagery, an encounter between ferocity and gentleness that had been depicted in countless paintings, drawings, jewels and wall hangings. But all the works of art that Worm had examined had one thing in common: judging by the length of the horns that he himself had measured and weighed, the unicorn was always portrayed as too small. The simple experiment of binding an accurate replica of a unicorn horn to a billy goat had proved that to carry a lengthy, twenty-pound horn would require more than just a ferocious nature: the horn would have to sprout from a broad forehead on a large head that sat in turn on a much bulkier body than anyone had ever envisaged, a fact that made the beast's invisibility even harder to explain. Worm began to make enquiries about the origins of the horns that were known to exist in the treasuries of cathedrals and palaces. It transpired that, with the exception of the unicorn horn encased in the sceptre of Elizabeth I, the Virgin Queen of England – which she had bought from a Muscovy trader for the price of a castle – the horns were all found in places where Icelanders had studied or traded, or merely stopped for a breather on their journeys to Rome or Jerusalem. The Flemish polymath Goropius Becanus, for example, claimed that the three horns he had examined in Antwerp in the middle of the sixteenth century had all come from Iceland, and Worm was aware that before the introduction of Lutheranism to Iceland, the leading men in that country had been in the habit of sending their sons to Antwerp to study the art of business.

The learned doctor was thrilled by this news, for he had confidants on the volcanic island, old colleagues and students from the University of Copenhagen, who would be able to confirm whether their inclement homeland fostered other land animals besides field mice and Arctic foxes; whether it was possible that unicorns trod the black sand wastes to the accompaniment of rumbling volcanoes and glaciers, and, if not, whether this ivory was found among the other flotsam and jetsam from distant lands that was washed ashore on Iceland's strands. But his old acquaintances could provide little in the way of answers. They thought it unlikely that such treasures were to be found in Iceland, at least they had never set eyes on them, and despite their repeated promises to ask this or that old fellow with a long memory, when their correspondent reminded them of the matter some months later, they had invariably forgotten all about it. In spite of the countless letters he had sent, he remained none the wiser about the possible export of unicorn horns from the colony in the north. But in addition to his importuning of Icelandic bishops, clerics and squires – his contacts were all pillars of society – Ole Worm had received permission from the Danish chancellery to perform a chemical analysis on one of the two horns in the possession of the realm. He conducted these experiments in secret as he did not wish to offend his brother-in-law and mentor, Professor Caspar Bartholinus, who in 1628 had published the book *De Unicorno* in which he proclaimed the healing powers of the horns which, due to their mysterious origin, were considered an efficacious remedy for epilepsy, melancholy, cramp, gout and other disorders, in addition to being an infallible antidote against snake bites and earthly poisons such as arsenic and sublimate. Various methods were used to administer the medicine, but the most common was to scrape the horn with a sharp knife and mix the resulting powder with wine which was then given to the patient to drink. In addition, it was not unknown for the thickest section at the base of the horn to be made into a cup, whose virtue was such that any unadulterated liquid poured into it would instantly be transformed into a healing draught, whereas if the drink was poisoned, a sweat would appear on the cup's outer rim. But these precious objects were only within the means of the rich and powerful who were, after all, always falling victim to poison. Ole Worm decided to conduct experiments on these properties: in a back room belonging to the apothecary Woldenberg, he gave healthy kittens arsenic to drink until they began to stagger and bleed from their mouths and nostrils, upon which they were administered unicorn's horn ground up in milk. They all died, as did the pigeons fed on corn soaked in chloride of mercury. But what the ever-curious Wormius did learn from his experiments with the horns was that in their internal structure and substance they resembled ivory rather than rhinoceros horn. His researches progressed no further until Jónas Pálmason the Learned set eyes on the royal treasure, a unicorn's horn set in a fragment of skull, and sank to the floor, overcome with hilarity.

Once Jónas and Worm had recovered from their laughter and refreshed themselves with blackcurrant juice (good for the kidneys) and spiced loaf (good for the bowels), it became apparent that Jónas was no less accomplished a natural historian than he was a runic scholar, and an experienced ivory-smith into the bargain, who had been engraving pictures on whale ivory and walrus tusks ever since he was young. He revealed that the object wrapped in velvet, far from being what it purported to be, was the tusk of the savage whale known as the narwhal, or 'corpse whale' because of its taste for drowned sailors, and Worm duly recorded the object in his workbook as 'Narwhal's Tusk'. The Icelanders had first encountered these horrid beasts when they founded a colony in Greenland around the year 1000 Anno Domini and soon began to export the tusks, labelling them as 'unicorn horns' according to the latest fashion. The Greenlanders and their middlemen in west Iceland grew fat on the profits of this secret commerce, which ensured the Greenlandic colony an advantageous balance of trade with foreign lands as well as laying the foundation for the wealth of the most powerful families in Iceland. The trade continued uninterrupted until the Greenlandic colony was abandoned a hundred years ago, in the year of Our Lord 1540. Narwhal tusks were now a rare commodity in the country, but people could expect to get a high price for them as long as belief in the existence of the unicorn persisted, so Dr Worm must promise not to tell his correspondents in Iceland who had spilt the beans. This promise was easily extracted. Jónas drew diagrams for Worm showing how the fish lay in the sea, wielding its tusk like a lance, and a comparison of these with the royal specimen convinced Worm that it was a narwhal skull with a tusk and nothing more. And so that day in the Museum Wormianum the unicorn's fate was sealed: a year after his meeting with Jónas Pálmason, Ole Worm published an epoch-making article on the similarity between narwhal tusks and unicorn horns. For the next three decades the brightest luminaries of Western philosophy wrangled over the existence of the fantastic horned beast with the goat's beard, horse's abdomen, pig's tail, antelope's head and elephant's feet, until the sceptics finally prevailed. Upon which the price of unicorn horns plummeted. This result was a remote but sweet revenge for Jónas the Learned, since many of his chief persecutors in Iceland were descended from unicorn merchants.

The professor's delight in his new amanuensis was such that he began to make plans for Jónas's permanent residence in Copenhagen. After consultation with Reverend Pálmi Gudmundur, who had received a satisfactory verdict in his lawsuit and was now able to return to Iceland to take up the position of curate at Hjaltastadur, it was decided that instead of going home with his son, Jónas should send for his wife Sigrídur to come to Denmark. Jónas was sixty-three years old by now and she fifty-seven; he would help Worm translate ancient texts and draw objects from his collection when required; she meanwhile could assist in the kitchens. A decent private chamber would be found for them in the upper servants' quarters and they would finally be allowed to live in peace after twenty years of being hounded from pillar to post. Jónas Pálmason's breast swelled with hope: although he himself had not spent any time out of doors in Copenhagen, Sigga would enjoy the novelties on display; the fireworks, the court finery and the elegant buildings would be balsam to her weary eyes.

On the May evening when he and Rector Worm shook hands on the plan, Jónas took from his pouch a small, dice-shaped box of seal-bone which contained his rarest possession, a blood-black crystal, yellow at the edges, which was at once a work of nature and a holy mystery. It was a kidney stone that had become trapped in Bishop Gudbrandur Thorláksson of Hólar's private member, which Jónas had with his own hand removed from said member according to the instructions preserved in the saga of the medieval doctor, Hrafn Sveinbjarnarson. Having split the penis like an uncooked sausage, he picked the stones out of the urinary tract before sewing the whole thing up again. The cleric's stone-afflicted body had given birth to three crystals, one of which Jónas had quietly pocketed and kept by him ever since. The bishop's gratitude had secured Pálmi Gudmundur a place at the school of divinity in Hólar (with the help of a document in Jónas's possession which proved that the bishop's son-in-law, Ari Magnússon of Ögur, had violated the king's law). Now, however, Jónas made a gift of the kidney stone to his friend Ole Worm in return for providing a roof over his and Sigrídur's heads.

The following day a handwritten sealed writ arrived from His Majesty King Christian IV, in which the king concurred with the University Council's verdict that Jónas Pálmason was not a practitioner of the black arts. Instead of acquitting him unconditionally, however, His Majesty referred the case to the court of the Althing at Thingvellir in Iceland and bade the Icelanders themselves formally revoke the sentence in the presence of the defendant.

Jónas the Learned was going home.

III

(Winter Solstice, 1637)

Evening has fallen on the shortest day of the year and, dear God, the longest night lies ahead. How many hours of light did I get? Two? Three? One? It was a dismal day, after a bad beginning. When morning finally came I was cheated of what meagre share of daylight I could hope for. Thick banks of cloud hung over the island, as low as could be, tinged black at the crown; a heavy, merciless weight, shedding neither rain nor snow. The dreariest kind of clouds, which drain one of vigour, clamping their iron-grey fists around one's skull, digging their talons deep into eyes and ears, forcing them into mouth and nose in an attempt to fill one's head with grey sleet, to burst it from within and crush it from without. With effortless strength they depress one's humour into the coldest wells of thought and imprison it there, but unlike the cloud of smoke that drives occupants of a burning house to the floor in the hope of snatching a breath of life-giving air, nothing awaits one at the bottom of that pit of despair but a mouthful of acrid yellow gall. There is no gleam of hope, no mercy to be found on this frozen tundra; the ground is as hard as stone underfoot, the frost reaches down to the very bedrock. The sea has frozen halfway from the island to the mainland and the ice is stained a dirty black following the sandstorm at Martinmas. Not that I can see the shore, for the mountains are as dark as the sky – assuming they are still there. What do I know? Damn the mountains. Above them hangs a pall of black gloom, like the lid of a narrow iron casket. So this day began, and it only grew worse. When the tangle of clouds finally began to unravel it was not the sun that appeared from behind them, no, it was the feeble glimmer of the moon. Was I supposed to be grateful? After all, light is light, is it not? Ah no, the cold moonlight was nothing but a bitter reminder of what I was missing: the winter sun. Her weak rays may lack the power to disperse the sea ice, waken the growing things in the soil or inspire the bunting to sing, yet even so her pallid face fills one's breast with faith in her ability to do these very things. A faith that warms the cockles of one's heart. Even more than the sunlight itself, it was this spark of hope that was denied to me. It was not as if I needed strong light to perform the chores that awaited me when I crawled out of my lair at noon; for those, even the moon's sullen grin was superfluous. What need had I to venture outside in the loathsome winter weather? Well, to empty my chamber pot of its paltry contents that had frozen solid in the night. Where little goes in, little comes out: no more than two droppings in this case, congealed in a single splash of piss. There are many reasons for this: firstly, I am such an old wreck nowadays that my bowels have become sluggish; secondly, in recent weeks the weather has been so stormy that I do not leave the hut unless it is unavoidable, and as I hardly move at all, I need less food; and thirdly, I have scarcely anything left to eat. And I have nothing with which to counter any of this: old age, the time of year or dearth of food. The sheet of ice has its beginning halfway down the beach and surrounds the whole island with its sudden creaks and eerie groans, pleated like one of the Lord Chief Justice's starched ruffs. On the beach all life has been scorched by the cold; the sand is as hard as stone, the seaweed withered. Haddock and cod lie under the furthest rim of the ice, if they have not frozen to death too, but I have neither the strength nor the nerve to go out there, lacking a boat. What would I do there anyway? Talk the fish up through the ice? I have little fishing tackle and am too frail to hack a hole in the ice for my line. There is nothing here for the gulls but the boulders on which they rest before resuming their search for food with feeble flaps of their wings and famished cries. Even if I had a piece of string to snare them with, I do not have any bait for my trap apart from the flesh on my own bones, because I am not going to start feeding scavengers from my scanty stores – all I have left to last me till spring is a bundle of dried trout, some soup bones, a bunch of dried dulse, half a bag of flour, the butter that has not yet been scraped off the sides of the barrel – and I hardly think it would be wise to habituate the gulls to the taste of myself. Not that such a thing would be necessary; I expect Master and Mistress Seamew already have plans to feast on my corpse if I freeze to death on one of my trips to empty my piss pot. Well, if that is how my life is to end, the pickings will make a meaner banquet than the gulls anticipate: I wish them good cheer. But the worst was still to come; this brutal day had yet to play its cruellest trick; God in His wisdom had resolved to test me still further. I had just started to chip away at the contents of my piss pot when I noticed that the moon seemed to have changed shape: its left-hand side was dented, like a cheek yielding before Famine's spectral finger. At first I assumed the heavy clouds were closing in on it again, and thought it a damned shame that they would not leave it to hang there in peace, but on closer inspection I noticed that the clouds had, if anything, thinned. I carried on banging the pot on a rock. Although there was little in it, I had to be careful not to bang it too hard as the wooden strakes had been eaten away by the urine and I could not afford to break it. Against the background of that hollow banging I watched as a quarter of the moon was gnawed away. Fear and trembling! Through my winter lethargy I grasped what was happening: a lunar eclipse. The moon, the only source of light meanly allotted to me in my solitary state on this gloomiest day of the year, was darkening. Behind me the sun crept as furtively as a fox beneath the rim of the horizon, casting the Earth's shadow over her wretched brother. In doing so she put us both in our place, reminding the moon that without her he was nothing but a dreary, lightless mountain of basalt, and ordering the beggar Jónas Pálmason to clear off back inside his hovel. Insignificant humans were not welcome at the heavenly bodies' cheerless family farce. If I stood there one minute longer with my nose pointing at the darkened moon, I would drop dead on the spot and be found in spring, lying there lifeless with my rigid hands still clamped round the piss pot. I saw now that this day no longer deserved the name; it would be better to tear it out of the calendar and file it where it belonged between the pages of Satan's black book as 'Night'. Obeying the command of the wrathful sun, I hastened inside, barred the door, crawled into the kitchen, put the chamber pot by the bed and lay down, pulling up the blanket and making the sign of the cross. And here I lie still. Oh, is it not just and true what those foreign mountebanks write in their many widely read travel accounts about the vileness and absurdity of Iceland, this condemned island of the dead – however much her educated citizens may revile and rant at them? Old Arngrímur Jónsson blew raspberries at such accounts in two books, both of which found their way into print; in one he included a portrait of himself, in the other a fine drawing of a monkey. Bishop Oddur Einarsson also compiled a book, of which copies can be found here and there, though minus illustrations; and Bishop Gísli, Oddur's son, has two small pamphlets in the making, although there is little enthusiasm for them. I have not read any of these counterblasts, for they are all in Latin, which I do not know, but I have no doubt they play fast and loose with the truth, being at the same time tediously written and dull to read, since none of these three is to the popular taste or known for his poetic skills. On the other hand, various titbits from the controversial travellers' tales have been passed on to me, though I have not seen any of them myself since the lords of our land place them on a par with murder. But even from these scraps I can tell that although, naturally, they get most things wrong, tell many lies, exaggerate and fill in the blanks with fantasy – indeed, wise men tell me that it is evident from their works that scarcely a man of them has ever set foot in this country – nevertheless one fact stands out from all their foolish nonsense: they come close to the truth when they state that Iceland is no paradise in winter: on the contrary, it is hell. The Englishman Thomas Nashe apparently says in his *Terrors of the Night*: 'Admirable (above the rest) are the incomprehensible wonders of the bottomless Lake Vetter, over which no fowl flies but is frozen to death, nor any man passeth but he is senselessly benumbed like a statue of marble.' Of course there is no lake in Iceland called 'Vetter', and there is precious little admirable about these horrors, and whether some of our larger lakes are bottomless I would not like to say. But what the foreign gentleman manages better than I, or any of my highly educated countrymen, is to describe the bitter helplessness and numbness I feel on this midwinter's day on the Corpse Strand, far from the sun. I know it, I am there. And so it is with all the far-fetched tales that wind up the Arngrímurs of this world with their uncouth exclamations about endless nights, burning snow, whales the size of mountains, trumpet blasts of the dead from volcanoes and icebergs, witches who can sell sailors a favourable wind or send their sons to the moon; in some strange way they come close to the stories that we ordinary, humble folk tell ourselves in an attempt to comprehend our existence here and make it more bearable. Now that I give it more thought, how do I know that there are no lakes here like those described by Master Nashe? None of Iceland's leading men were willing to pay me to explore this land; they turned a deaf ear to the news I gathered about silver sand, veins of gold and nests of gems. No, they are too busy growing rich on what this libertine Earth has to offer, passing corrupt judgements, hindering honest men from supporting their offspring, breaking up their families, cutting off their fingers and ears. In the same passage in Gentleman Thomas's book we can read: 'It is reported that the Pope long since gave them a dispensation to receive the sacrament in ale, insomuch as for their incessant frosts there, no wine but was turned to emayle as soon as ever it came amongst them', and also 'they have ale that they carry in their pockets like glue, and ever when they would drink, they set it on the fire and melt it.' He who is omniscient knows that in this miserable hour it would be a comfort to me to be able to reach into my pocket and fetch out a beakerful of warm, consoling ale. But here, alas, old Tommy is telling a flat lie.

—

WHITE WHALE: *from this creature is derived the proverb that 'the white whale seldom fails on the fishing grounds', for it is considered very wise and can often be found near fishermen, although it hides itself from view and rarely breaks the surface. The story goes that once all the crew but one were asleep on a shark-fishing vessel when a white whale surfaced and stayed beside the ship. The vigilant man reacted quickly and struck it with a* *club. When the rest of the crew awoke, they warned that he could expect retaliation, and heeding their warning, the man took to the hills. He stayed away from the sea for thirteen years. But at the end of that time, believing the white whale to be dead, he returned to the same fishing ground. A white whale appeared at once and seized him alone from the ship, and neither fish nor man was ever seen again. This is the origin of the saying about a man with a long memory: 'he holds a grudge longer than a white whale'.*

—

The kitchen is the smallest room in the hut; it is easiest to keep warm in here – if one can call it easy, or warm, for that matter. To fit the bed in here I had to pull the frame off the doorways between hall and living room, and between kitchen and hall. I did not replace the frames: they went on the fire. This is poor workmanship, I know – the hut will fall in on my head – but I needed the warmth after all my efforts. The kitchen doorway proving still too narrow, I had to break the legs off the bed in order to manhandle it through at a slant, and once it was inside I found it impossible to replace them, so I burnt them too. And since the base of the bed frame proved too long for the kitchen, I had to prop it up against the wall to the right of the door and jam the other end hard against the stones of the hearth. As a result, my bed tilts rather, meaning either my head is halfway up the wall and my feet by the hearth, or else my feet are up and my head is down, so when the pot is on the fire either my head boils and my feet freeze, or vice versa. I am continually turning round in bed, spinning back and forth like a top, which does my rheumatism no good at all. Thus I huddle by the hearth like a stay-at-home hero, edited out of my own story, too thoroughly buried and forgotten to be called on to perform unexpected feats of courage in a far-off kingdom. Yet I proved a useful guest in the realm of that busy monarch, Christian IV. Last summer I returned from Denmark in triumph, bearing a royal writ signed by His Majesty's own hand and witnessed by many long-tailed seals, in which he enjoined his subjects, my countrymen, to accede to his wishes and revoke the foolish, brutal sentence they had passed on me at their libertine court in the mud of Thingvellir in 1631. With his own hand he had attached to his letter a sincere recommendation by the most learned men in the Danish realm, who had subjected me to a whole day of the strictest interrogation under the guidance of their rector and most erudite principal, Ole Worm. That throng of luminaries had gathered in the University Council known as the Consistorium, which for the infallibility and fairness of its judgements is respected and admired by all the nobles of that land, and thus these most skilled practitioners in the art of learning confirmed that Jónas Pálmason of Strandir had done nothing more heinous than compile an anthology of harmless ancient lore, of uneven quality to be sure, as with any human endeavour, and most of it outmoded, but the man himself far from being a sorcerer was a curious and diligent scholar of the arts of the mind and hand, although unschooled. Clutching this fine testimonial and the writ signed by the king, I boarded ship at Copenhagen last spring, confident that once home on Icelandic soil I could expect justice to be restored. But my happiness proved short-lived, for among my fellow passengers were the emissaries of that slanderous forked tongue that had so softly licked the ears of certain men in Denmark the autumn before and had me thrown in gaol. Their ringleader was the nephew of Sheriff Ari Magnússon, easily recognised by the family trait, a birthmark at the corner of his left eye. These little vipers won over the young captain who had been commissioned to carry me home, tricking him into believing that I was to blame for the winds that stirred up the sea and drove huge waves at his ship. They worked so well on his simple soul that when we reached the coast of Iceland near Rosmhvalsnes and sea devils, ratfish, malign mermen and other monsters raised a six-day storm that prevented us from going either forward or back, the captain, in the belief that I was stirring up the sea by sorcery, ordered his crew to throw me overboard. But no sooner had they dragged me up on the gunwale than the storm abruptly subsided, so there was no need to drown me on that occasion. After this the poor merchant and his crew were more convinced than ever that I was a sorcerer, but so in awe were they of my powers that I was left in peace for the remaining two days of the voyage. Naturally, it did not occur to any of them that blessed Providence might have intervened to save them from killing an innocent man. The vipers, meanwhile, slithered in among the coils of rope on deck and lay low until we reached land. The merchant vessel had barely cast anchor in Hafnarfjord before the slander-mongers put out a boat and rowed to shore. This did not bode well. Before I knew it, the governor's executioner was being ferried out to the ship, accompanied by a second man and a neck iron, with the obvious intention of arresting me. I fled the executioner by swarming up the mast, from where I yelled that I would rather jump in the sea than set foot in my native land in chains. At which point it transpired that those same crew members who had been most eager to throw me overboard now wished by all means to prevent me from drowning of my own accord. Taking courage from the presence of the executioner, they chased me up the mast, dragged me down on deck and held me fast while he clamped the iron round my neck. And so I went ashore chained like a savage dog, which was a fitting preliminary to the brutal treatment that my tormenters had in store for me: they clapped me in irons, tied me backwards on an ancient mare and made me ride in front so that whenever we approached a farm on our way to Thingvellir the dogs would get wind of me first and run barking and baying around the mare, to be followed by a pack of crowing urchins and adults who abused me with ignorant insults and cat calls. Yet none of them knew of what crime the alleged felon was accused. When we reached court, the judges flouted the royal request, ignored the

University Council's words and confirmed their former sentence of outlawry. What made it all the more poignant for me was that the judges called themselves king's men, a number were divines and others professed themselves Christians, and many of them had on their travels to Copenhagen been generously received at the home of the hospitable Worm and continued to enjoy his kindness after their return to Iceland. I had with my own eyes seen how these false friends plagued the learned doctor with letters importuning him to acquire for them all kinds of perishable items, from aqua vitae to Sunday breeches, or to mention their name at court, or to provide medical advice for their own or their mothers-in-law's haemorrhoids, their wives' toothache and their children's constipation – all of which ailments stemmed from the attempts of these homespun 'aristocrats' to ape the lifestyle of court in the Icelandic countryside, with the attendant idleness, intemperance and indulgence in sweetmeats in the Danish fashion. It was not enough that they required him to turn a blind eye to the indolence of their sons who were supposed to be studying at the university – the funds that were wasted on paying for those oafish gallants' carousing and unheard-of extravagance in clothes would have been better spent if the Church could have commandeered them for the herd of barefoot beggars who were daily turned away from the kitchen doors at the childhood homes of these finely tricked-out drunkards – no, as if that were not enough, the most importunate among these petitioners actually expected Master Worm to take the time to compose obituary poems for them, though to lighten his burden they themselves provided the praise. In return for his trouble they sent him old books, healing stones and natural objects that seldom arrived in one piece: maggoty bird skins, rotten skates, shells and eggs in a thousand fragments, and stones of invisibility, clumsily faked. Preceptor Worm and I used to make fun of all this rubbish when I visited him, laughing aloud, the university man and the poet. Yet he put up with this one-sided trade with the Icelanders because just occasionally they would by accident send him something of value, such as the gaming piece of whale ivory, pretty old and decently carved, which is not surprising since it was a gift from that worthy fellow Magnús Ólafsson of Laufás. Although Ole Worm's treacherous correspondents included honest men, like my Laufás kinsmen, none of this better group was among the judges who treated me so scandalously for a second time. If anything, their hatred was even more venomous than before as they were smarting over the fact that the University Council's verdict declared in effect that their judgement of me had been ill-founded and deserved to be thrown out. Moreover, my friendship with the learned doctor had filled their hearts with envy and fear that I would tell him the truth about them: like the prankster who pisses on the calves after being flogged for throwing stones at the cows, they chose to compound their disgrace. Thus they reinforced my sentence by adding a clause that until someone was willing to give me passage abroad, I was to languish in irons in the dungeon at the governor's residence in Bessastadir, in the full knowledge that no captain would be found for that passage any more than last time and I would have to end my days in the black hole, a prospect they found sweet. There I relived my nightmare of six years earlier, though now there was no Brynjólfur Sveinsson with his gentle touch. To the accompaniment of mocking jeers from the crowd I was tied on the mare's back again and the executioner was just about to strike her when his master, the governor's deputy Jens Söffrinson, steward of Bessastadir, called for silence. He beseeched the court to show mercy and spare him the burden of housing an ugly customer like Jónas Pálmason. The deputy's words led to a good deal of tittering and sniggering, with accompanying hand gestures, head-tossing and tutting. However, once everyone had remembered their hands and wiped the froth from their lips, they acceded to his request and back I was sent to this island.

—

And there she lay, in the patch of heather beside the path leading to our hut, a plaything of the wind and weather: my wife, Sigrídur Thórólfsdóttir, now nothing but a heap of black rags. Throwing down my belongings, I ran to her, fell on my knees and flung my arms around her, crying: 'Sigga, Sigga!' Only to recoil at once, for a chill emanated from her body like the draught from a passageway. I raced in the direction of the landing place, waving and calling for help, but the lad who had ferried me to the island was out of earshot by now, bending to his oars off the north bank, and either did not or feigned not to see me. Running back, I took Sigga in my arms again, pressing her against me, but under the shawls she was nothing but bones. I struck my brow with my clenched fist: my God, oh my God! The damned swine had betrayed her; no one had helped her with the autumn chores or bothered to bring her supplies before Christmas or cared to see how the old woman on Gullbjörn's Island was coping. I consigned them all to hell. Her shawl was pulled down over her nose and nothing could be seen of her face but the pursed lips and stubborn chin. I drew the cloth gently back over her brow; the bluish-yellow flesh was icy cold yet seemed unblemished, apart from a sprig of flowering thyme that sat fast in her right cheek. But where were her eyes? Had the ravens been at her? I fumbled at her eyelids; thank God, there was substance under them; I had been misled by their black appearance. I wept. It began to rain, then stopped. I wept on: for now I had killed my Sigga too. Evening fell and the rain started again. I carried her into the hut, laid her body on the bed in the living room, knelt down beside her and begged her to forgive me for all the wrongs I had done her, both great and small: for the trials she had been forced to endure on account of my obsessive curiosity and delving; the collecting mania that had filled all our chests with unidentifiable berries, fool's gold and deadly poisonous plants, and books in languages that neither of us could read, while a cold wind blew among the empty cooking pots; the endless gabbling of elves and trolls; the evening I spoke harshly to her in front of the children; the hare-brained schemes and worthless conceits my mind constantly spewed forth that were to cost us so dear; the prospect of fame that dragged us from place to place, constantly on the move, from one side of the country to the other, only to end up in a bottomless well of debt to the very people who were supposed to make me rich, with the result that our home had to be broken up yet again. I begged her forgiveness for the deplorable sufferings I had caused her through my meddling in affairs too deep for a poor poet, by which I had provoked the enmity of powerful men with whom I could not contend, failing to realise that they were jackals, not lions, that they would not be satisfied until they had severed my head from my body. The silence that followed was overwhelming, unbroken this time by the quick retort with which Sigrídur had in recent years responded to any discourse of mine, regardless of topic:

'That's the sort of nonsense that got us here in the first place!'

Whenever I heard those words all the wind would leave my sails; they seemed to strike at the very root of my impotence. It was only too true that my nonsense had driven us here and there, hither and thither, back and forth. We had been forced to dwell in so many '*here*'s against our will on our constant flight from my enemies, from the predatory silver-plated claws that clutched after me and my loved ones. Me and all I held dear. There were spies at every turn, ready to betray a poor vagabond in the hope that his powerful foes would throw them a morsel. Ah, Judas's pleasure was short-lived and his remorse scalded and stung, but these scoundrels had no conscience; they bragged of getting the outlaw Jónas the Learned arrested for their own amusement and a reward of thirty brass farthings. My children's despair is still etched in my memory as they watched their father being thrown in the mud, beaten and belaboured with fists and clubs, before being flung, helplessly, head first into the black hole of prison. I can still hear the poor little darlings' sad wails as they embraced one another outside the prison wall, laying their tender ears to the stone in the hope of hearing their father say that everything would be all right. On the other side of the wall I writhed in my chains, throwing up my hands and calling out just that: 'All will be well, dear children, with God's help all will be well, when the Lord hears your prayers and my pleas, all will be well.' Yet things did not improve, they only got worse. I ran my fingers gently over Sigga's brow, down her nose and cheek, avoiding the sprig of thyme. The last time I heard her refer to 'us', she meant only herself and her old man, me, the two sad wretches on Gullbjörn's Island. But once it meant 'the two of us and our four children', then 'us two and our three children', and later 'us two and our two children', until finally it was only 'us two and Little Gudmundur', for only the eldest, Pálmi Gudmundur, survived into adulthood, benefiting no doubt from being named after the good Bishop Gudmundur Arason. His brothers and sisters all fell to the scythe, slender shoots, withered before their time. One never becomes used to it. The ewe runs faster than the lamb, the swan takes to the air sooner than the cygnet, the char darts through the water quicker than the minnow, and little children tire before their parents. Father and mother look on helplessly as their babies die. 'That's the sort of nonsense that got us here!' The speaker of that bitter truth had departed this life, the word 'us' now referred to me alone, and in that dark hour I would gladly have given my own life to have heard it once more from her living lips. A tear gleamed in the corner of her left eye. For a moment I was ecstatic with joy – Sigga was not dead, she had merely swooned from hunger; I would nurse her, cook medicinal herbs for her, rub the warmth back into her stiff hands, help her walk over the rough ground until she recovered her strength – but my world grew dark again when I realised it was only a tear that had fallen from my own eye on to hers. Sigrídur lay on her side with her legs drawn up under her, as if taking a nap, for thus had her body stiffened. I climbed into bed behind her, laying my arm over her body, resting my cheek against the back of her neck; her shawl smelt of moss campion and crowberry. I whispered:

'So you have gone now to the kingdom beyond the clouds, beyond sun and moon and sky, to the land where all grief is comforted with eternal radiant mercy at the footstool of Christ. Where your children will greet you, running to their mother with outstretched arms ...'

I could say no more, my throat tightened on the last word. If our dead children had been allowed to live they would have been grown-up by now, with many children of their own. They would have given old Grandpa Jónas and Grandma Sigga shelter in their homes; for he who has once dwelt in his mother's body and his father's heart is bound to provide them with a roof over their heads in their old age. But it was not to be, it will never be. I was seized by a bitter rage. Clenching my fists, I prayed:

'Dear God, take that black-hearted knave Nightwolf Pétursson and give back to me little Hákon, who was always as gentle as a girl; merciful Father, take Ari Magnússon of Ögur and return to me quick-handed Berglind, who inherited her father's gift for carving; heavenly Creator, take that foul-tongued slanderer, Reverend Gudmundur Einarsson, and give me back the little lad Klemens, with one moss-green eye and one blue; dear Lord, take the whole legion of good-for-nothings who every day outlive their victims, sprawling in their high seats and thrones, gorging themselves on meat, dripping with grease, from the livestock that grew fat on the green grass in meadows tended with diligence by innocent, God-fearing souls; congratulating themselves on having stripped this man of his livelihood and that woman of her breadwinner – when they can speak between ill-gotten mouthfuls; enjoying to a great old age the fruits of the wicked deeds they committed during their days on Earth with the blessing of bishops, and convinced that the despicable acts that they refer to as "a good day's work in the Lord's vineyard" will have paid for their place in Heaven; dear God, snatch them away and do with them what you will, but give back to me Sigrídur Thórólfsdóttir, a pious woman, a loving wife and a caring mother who never asked for anything for herself but prayed for mercy and good fortune for friends and strangers alike.'

These terrible curses poured in torrents from my mouth. They were so dire that when I came to my senses I hoped that the good Lord in His mercy and deep understanding of human frailty would pretend that His great all-hearing ears had been closed in that dark hour. As yet He has not brandished His rod of punishment over my head – indeed, what more could He do to me? I held Sigga's withered hands, feeling every sinew and knuckle, tracing the bones with my fingertips, and the sunken flesh between them, for she had starved a long time before she died. In spite of my attempts to dissuade her she had insisted on staying behind on the island. But how could a lone female survive a whole winter on this cursed rock? Not even the resourceful Sigrídur Thórólfsdóttir could do that. And who knows what will become of me? She had clasped her hands in her hour of death and I found with my forefinger that she was holding something between them. I rose up on my elbow; the corner of a piece of brown cloth peeped from her fist. The cloth turned out to be wrapped round a gift from our friend Peter the Pilot, the confessor and helmsman on the whaler *Nuestra Señora del Carmen*. It was a holy relic: four little wood shavings, no larger than nail clippings, reddish in hue.

—

> **AIR SHIP:** *a strange event occurred in the western quarter: a rope with an anchor on the end fell from the sky and caught in the church pavement. The whole congregation could see and touch it when they came out of the service. After a while a man came down the rope and tried to free the anchor, but when people touched him he became as weak as a fish out of water and the mark of death was straight away seen upon him. The minister forbade anyone to touch the man again and ordered them to free the anchor. Then everything was hauled up, man, rope and anchor, and never seen again.*

—

They came gliding over the sea like cathedrals under their white sails: church ships, launched from a southern shore, their three masts bearing fluttering Christian flags and banners, their prows decorated with artfully painted figureheads, glaring with admonishment at any sea monster that dared to venture near, and crosses carved on both bows, while from the stern rose a statue of the Virgin Mary with arms outstretched in a maternal embrace that encompassed both vessel and crew. On their sterns they bore the names of the most holy and beneficent churches in their homeland: *Nuestra Señora de la Paz*, *Nuestra Señora de la Estrella* and *Nuestra Señora de la Inmaculada Concepción* – and when the wind stood from the sea one could hear the ship's bell singing:

'Peace, star, immaculate ... Peace, star ...'

Sigrídur and I had only been living at Litla-Vík for two months when we saw them coming in from the sea. It was early summer of the year 1613. She was tending to the ewes, I sat in the smithy, supposedly carving a picture story on a bull's horn, a commission I had already been paid for and which was now overdue, but in fact struggling my way through a collection of *Aesop's Fables* in German. Pálmi Gudmundur sat in the smithy doorway, playing at piling up some bones that I had painted in different colours for him. Then Sigga came running in, grabbed up the boy in her arms and called to me to come and see something rather remarkable. We stood on top of the farm mound, shielding our eyes with our hands. The sight was remarkable indeed; there was no 'rather' about it. I raised my brows and looked at Sigga enquiringly; she was smiling dreamily. I was greatly relieved, for she had been reluctant to move here from Ólafseyjar – although she had not exactly been happy there, particularly after the locals cheated me of my fee for laying the ghost of Geirmundur Hell-skin, claiming falsely that I had promised to find his buried treasure too – but I had managed to persuade her that we would be better off in the place where my fame was greatest, that is, my birth district of Strandir, bounded to the west by the Snjáfjöll coast. Yes, the marvellous spectacle floating out there on the summery sea boded well for our sojourn here. But when it became clear that these wondrous craft were heading out of sight, east round the headland and into the neighbouring fjord, we agreed that early next morning we would follow them. We set out on horseback, riding beasts given to us by my benefactors; I carrying our little boy in front of me.

Our eagerness to see the ships was so great that it seemed to infect the horses, which bounded along with such lightness of foot that before we knew it we had reached Reykjafjord. But no sooner had we arrived than we began to have misgivings. There were fires burning all over the place and when we neared the farm, it became apparent that all the loose furnishings had been piled up and set alight. The buildings stood empty, evidently abandoned in haste, for pots and other household utensils lay broken in the kitchen and various other small objects were strewn around the living room and passageways. Everything indicated that the fair vessels were sailing under false pretences, that they had brought destruction and slavery to the inhabitants. Sigrídur sat rigid in her saddle, gripped by dread, Pálmi Gudmundur hid his face in my chest and I had to fight back my tears, not from fear but because it seemed such a miserable end to our expedition. We decided to turn back. Then Pálmi Gudmundur burst out laughing. He pointed up the hillside, giggling:

'Fuddy man ...!'

Quite right; in the hayfield above the farm lay a pale bundle, of human appearance, furnished with both arms and legs, though not in the right places. I dismounted, placed the boy in Sigrídur's arms and went to take a look at this novelty. It turned out to be an unfortunate old lady who had caught her petticoat on a jutting piece of stone while climbing over the wall. She had been hanging there with her legs in the air since the day before. I released the poor dear and turned her the right way up, and once she had recovered her wits she was able to tell us the truth about the wrecked and abandoned settlement. When they saw the approaching ships the locals had panicked, and to prevent the supposed corsairs from getting anything for their pains, they had smashed and destroyed everything they could, burning their belongings or sinking them in bogs, before running away to hide among the stony wastes and moors. So great had been the panic that she herself had been left behind, hanging upside down like a nightdress on a washing line. When questioned, the old woman was fairly certain that although she had been watching them from the wrong way up, the supposed corsairs had held their course due south, sailing on towards Steingrímsfjord. This was the first indication we had of how the arrival of great ocean-going ships could terrify our neighbours in that district. At around nine o'clock that evening we rode down off the moors into the Selárdalur Valley. Out on the fjord before us the magnificent craft lay at anchor. A tent had been pitched in the hayfield belonging to Reverend Ólafur of Stadur, from which carried a delicious smell of roasting meat, accompanied by the lively sound of musical instruments and voices with a strange inflexion. They were Basques, come from Spain to try their luck at harpooning whales in the Icelandic fjords. In the following weeks the new arrivals set about building a whaling station. It would appear that the ships had accommodated a whole village in their bellies, for in no time at all there arose a harbour and forge, kitchen huts and laundries, timber and rope workshops and ovens for rendering oil, built of wonderfully regular bricks. I paid Reverend Ólafur frequent visits to observe how they conducted the whaling and rendered the oil. The minister, who was on good terms with the whalers, willingly showed them to the hunting grounds, for he said it was a kindness on their part to cull the monsters, since the Icelanders themselves had lost the knowledge of how to harpoon whales. It was sheer pleasure to watch how nimbly the Basques killed the beasts, with a combination of cunning, daring and enviable skill. There was often good cheer among us on shore as we watched the harpooners' small boats rocking on the red foaming crests of the waves while the titans wallowed in their own blood. The news quickly spread that the Spaniards only made use of the animals' blubber, and now the foolish people who had made themselves destitute by destroying their farms when the ships arrived began to flock to the station. The whalers showed great generosity, selling the whale meat, with the minister as middleman, for whatever small items the locals had to barter, such as stockings and bone buttons, which saved the lives of the hapless beggars. Most notable of all, however, was the visit by the new sheriff of the West Fjords, the young Hamburg-educated Ari Magnússon. After inspecting the station and questioning the foreigners and locals about their trade, he struck a deal with the captain of the Basque fleet, Señor Juan de Argaratte, that the fee for whaling should be a tenth part of each catch, to be paid to the sheriff's office in barrels of whale oil or their equivalent value in silver. It was a bargain to the satisfaction of both, but the Spaniards asked the Minister of Stadur to look after their copy of the licence, as it would be best placed with him should different captains sail to the whaling station the following year. Seventeen whales were caught that summer and the whalers were happy men. Come Michaelmas they dismantled the station and put out to sea. All reached home safely and their voyage was celebrated throughout the Basque country, where the news soon spread that in the far northern oceans off Iceland there was an inexhaustible supply of whales. In May of 1614, twenty-six whaling ships put out to sea from many different places on the north coast of Spain, though after an attack by English pirates only ten ships reached their destination. As before, the whalers set up camp and built their rendering ovens in Steingrímsfjord, though some occupied the bays and coves further north on the West Fjords peninsula. The friendly relations between the foreigners and locals continued; good service was provided and there was plenty of trading. The farmers, who had better wares to barter than the year before, were able to lay in stores of whale meat for the winter, dried or cured in brine, while in return the Spaniards received live sheep and calves, warm milk and fresh butter. Then Reverend Ólafur of Stadur died. His funeral was a memorable affair. The service held for him in his own church was Lutheran, but outside the Basques sang a Catholic mass for their benefactor. The service was led by Peter the Pilot, a Frenchman from the fleet captain Juan de Argaratte's ship, *Nuestra Señora del Carmen*, and he gave me permission to attend the mass. But because such heathen popish practices had not been seen in Iceland for a lifetime, it caused a mixture of scandal and fear. There was a great deal of coming and going from the church. Men pleaded the call of nature but then sat with their breeches round their ankles by the churchyard wall; they may have had difficulty in emptying their bowels but they had none in using their eyes. When they went back into church they made a great show of shuddering and banned their wives and children from going outside lest they be corrupted by the heretics' wicked ways. But not everyone had turned up in Stadur to pay their respects to the peace-maker, Reverend Ólafur. While the perfumed smoke rose from the Catholic priest's incense, some crofters had made their way to a cove further down the fjord and were busy stealing meat from a half-flensed whale that the Basques kept on the beach there. With that the peace was at an end and there was no one left to hold back the rabble but the Sheriff of Ögur. He, however, ignored the captains' complaints about the theft of meat, calling them 'lying heathens', for he had a scheme by which to make a better profit from the foreigners than he had done before. That coming winter Ari Magnússon intended to ask for the hand of Kristín, daughter of Bishop Gudbrandur of Hólar, and in order to be a worthy match he needed to increase his means substantially. The office of sheriff had provided leaner pickings than he had anticipated and although the whale tithe was considerable, it was not enough. The master of Ögur now banned all trade with the whalers, citing the same king's law that he himself had broken when he made a deal with the Basques over the whaling licence. At the same time he began to spread tales of their overbearing behaviour. For their voyage south they were forced to buy provisions from him alone. The whale meat he received from them in return for his sheep and dairy products he sold on to the common people at a vastly inflated price. This trade was resented by everyone except the man responsible.

—

A sledgehammer, three nails, a tree trunk and a crosspiece. When did a skilled craftsman first fiddle with a nail between his fingers, then happen to glance at the hammer that hung heavily at his side and see not the carpentry job in front of him but his brother nailed to a cross? What fisherman first toyed with the idea that it would be an excellent thing to stick large and small hooks in a man's flesh? What blacksmith first raised his glowing tongs from the fire and was filled with the urge to crush his sister's breast? What was he called, the horse-breaker who first used his whip on the back of the errand boy or lent his unbroken beasts to the authorities to tear the limbs from living people? What natural historian sees in water and fire the means by which to drown or burn a person, sees in the wind and plants the means to kill him by thirst or poison? Who first thought of employing all these useful objects to torture their fellow men to death? And why are they so easily converted into lethal instruments in the hands of man? Why may a knife not simply be a knife for carving wood, for slicing mutton from the bone or harvesting angelica? Why does the sharp blade invariably find an easy path to the jugular vein of one's fellow man? And how can the bloody instruments of murder then return to the world of practical use? Nobody knows, least of all me. One can still find tools in the Strandir district that today play an indispensable role in people's lives but twenty-two years ago were used for unspeakable atrocities, like the men who wielded them. Auger, awl, shovel, axe and spade, all turned to weapons in their hands. I am assailed by such terrible images of my Basque friends' fate that they heat up the inside of my head like flames in a furnace. Flinging off the sheepskin, I roll out of bed on to the kitchen floor, clamber to my feet and run out of the hut in nothing but my shirt and stockings. The winter night administers an icy slap of snow and for one blessed moment the searing memories subside. Only to flare up again with tenfold force, and over the unbearable, ghastly scenes I hear sung the words of 'The Spanish Ballad' that my old friend Sorcery-Láfi composed in the New Year of 1615 at the instigation of Ari Magnússon, who then sent his poet out to recite this travesty at evening entertainments throughout the district. Which that wretch Láfi did in his squeaky, insistent voice, sucking on his blackened teeth between verses:

Wherever they go these villains are always the
same,
rustling cattle and stealing sheep is their game,
and not so much as a penny they'll leave
to your name.

Filching butter and flour and every fish that we own;
the poor man's flesh was stripped from his bone,
while the frost hardened and wind did moan.

Aghast at these antics men and women did gaze
but fearing the tyrants, no protest dared raise;
'tis shocking to see how such wickedness pays.

Thus the big man of Ögur incited poor Láfi to blow on the flames of the locals' prejudice and hatred of Spaniards. If the whalers ever returned to the West Fjords, they would have nowhere to turn for their trade but to the tyrant himself. And so often were the polemical verses recited that by the beginning of summer people had come to believe them better than their own stories of fair dealings with the foreign heroes of the deep. Alas, at the beginning of June three whaling ships reached land after a perilous journey through the sea ice which still loomed off shore although the almanac showed it to be summer. At first the odd farmer ventured to trade with the Basques but this soon stopped because wherever Ari Magnússon went he sniffed at people's cooking pots and the smell of whale meat was hard to disguise. The captains of the two smaller ships, Domingo de

Arguirre and Esteban de Tellaria, put up with this state of affairs, having no doubt experienced harsher conditions in their whaling stations on Jan Mayen. But the third captain was on his first trip to Iceland and found it hard to understand why his fellows and the servile local peasants should respect Ari's ban on trade. His name was Martinus de Villefranca, a young man of great promise who had taken over *Nuestra Señora del Carmen* on this voyage. To support him he had my good friend Peter the Pilot, but no doubt he took the occasional sheep from the mountainside in spite of the pilot's warnings. Martinus was not only handsome but unusually hardy and did what no other captain had done before: he went out himself on the harpoon boats. So the summer passed, with few whales, frequent accidents and monotonous fare. But the first real test of the master of Ögur's new dictate came that autumn when the whalers prepared to return home to the Basque country with their meagre haul. By then the weather resembled midwinter, ice lay right up to the head of the fjord and for weeks the sky had been upholstered in black from dawn to dusk. I wade through the snow from the door of my hut, abandoning the little shelter that the hovel provides against the north wind, and trudge down to the foot of the mound where the buffeting is even worse, though it would take more, much more, to blow out the fires of my nightmare. The blizzard lashes me from without; a bonfire consumes me from within. The Tuesday after Saint Matthew's Day, that is the nineteenth of September, the whaling ships assembled in the fjord which is now known as Reykjafjord, Smoky Fjord, but used to be called Skrímslafjord or Monster Fjord. There the captains divided up the haul and prepared their vessels for the homeward voyage. Although the catch could have been better, the fishermen were glad that the season was over and singing carried across the water from their ships towards dawn. Then the wind began to pick up and blew into a terrible tempest. During the night icebergs had drifted into the path of Esteban's and Domingo's vessels and before they could prevent them their ships broke their moorings and were driven by the icebergs towards the cliffs where their hulls crashed together. Nevertheless, by quick thinking the veteran captains managed to free their vessels from one another and eventually made it out to sea. The young Martinus, on the other hand, succeeded in raising his anchor and sailing down the fjord, but there he had to admit defeat and his great ship drifted out of control before the incredible wind, running aground on a stony beach where it rocked to and fro until the timbers of the hull eventually gave way under the strain and split with a loud groan. First the helm broke, then the ship was holed below the waterline and the sea poured in. The crew members pulled out their prayer books and prayed aloud with much shedding of tears. When Ari of Ögur heard what had happened he sounded the trumpet for battle against the shipwrecked men, ordering the farmers to take part at their own expense, against the promise of a share in the booty as a reward for each man they overcame. I alone of the Strandir men excused myself from the call-up, claiming that I had business south on the Snæfellsnes peninsula and would rather pay a fine for shirking the fray than let down the man who awaited me there. I lacked the courage to condemn the campaign as a heinous crime, but my action was enough to earn me threats and curses from the commander, who later made sure they all came true. Naturally Ari would have had me killed there and then had he known that following the death of Reverend Ólafur I had become custodian of the contract that he had made with the whalers, whom he had first cheated by deceitful wiles and now intended to deprive of both life and property. While the Basques struggled ashore in the dire conditions, some swimming or dog-paddling among the wreckage, others crawling on to the ice and razor-sharp rocks, the peasants armed themselves with tools, calling them weapons, and set out to meet the shipwrecked men. They caught Peter the Pilot first, along with a small group who had sought shelter in an abandoned fisherman's hut. They were ambushed in their sleep; Peter's head was resting on a psalter when it was smashed by a hammer blow, followed by a thrust from a knife through the heart and into the spine. Beside the pilot lay his burly companion, Lazarus, who, woken by the thud of the blow, tried to escape. He was slashed across the kneecaps, then set on by all who could reach him, yet he managed to keep them busy for quite a while. In an inner room they found the barber, stoker and washer boy, whom they also hacked to pieces. After that the bodies were stripped of their clothes and laid naked on stretchers. It was then that two objects were discovered on Peter's breast, the holy relics and his crucifix, which the warriors claimed were instruments of black magic, and even though they had failed to save him, none of them dared touch them. The dead were carried to the edge of a cliff, where they were lashed together and their naked, bloody corpses were sunk in the deep like heathens rather than poor innocent Christian men. When a great fork of lightning in the likeness of a sword struck the mountain, the leader declared that his followers should construe it as a sign of victory. After sailing back up and across the sound, in a tempest so fierce that it was barely possible to stay afloat, the mob reached the deserted farm where Martinus de Villefranca had taken refuge. He could be seen through the window, sitting beside a small fire with some of his men, while the rest were in the main room around a larger fire, over which they were drying their clothes. A man was set to guard every window and door, and when the leader gave the signal, many shots were fired inside. Martinus was heard to cry that he had not been aware that his crimes were so great that he and his men deserved to be shot down. Among the war band was the Minister of Snjáfjöll, Reverend Jón 'the Ghost-father', who was made to address the captain in Latin. In the end Martinus emerged from the hut, crawling on his knees with his hands in the air, and with tear-soaked face thanked Master Ari Magnússon for granting him and his men quarter. At that moment a man leapt forward with a great axe and struck at Martinus, aiming for his neck but hitting his collar bone instead and making only a small gash. Recoiling violently from the blow, Martinus took to his heels and fled from the hut down to the sea. It looked as if he was lying on the waves, stroking his head with one hand and his thigh with the other, swimming sometimes on his back, sometimes with arms whirling in the air, sometimes on his front, turning his head from side to side. A boat was launched with great palaver, containing men, weapons and stones, to defeat this Viking. When Martinus saw this he swam further out to sea, chanting in Latin all the while. Many thought it a wonder to hear his skill at singing. Those in the boat chased him with grim determination but he swam like a seal or fish, though one man boasted of having struck him with a spear while he was diving under the keel. Only when a farmer's boy managed to hit the swimmer on the forehead with a stone did his strength at last fail, and not until then. He was towed to the beach and stripped of all his clothes. As the man lay stark naked on the sand, eyes closed and groaning, one of the heroes stabbed him with his knife, cutting him in one slash from breastbone to groin. Martinus jerked violently, coiled up, then managed to get up on all fours, at which his guts fell out and after that he moved no more. The war band roared with laughter and many jostled close to see the man's insides but their view was obscured by the blood. Afterwards Martinus's hacked-apart body was sunk in the sea. At that the storm dropped, giving way to a calm which men attributed to the power of the foreign necromancer's body. Now an assault was made on the remaining Basques, after which none of the shipwrecked men from *Nuestra Señora del Carmen* had any need to beg for quarter. Guards were placed on all the exits and a hole was made in the turf roof. The sheriff's younger brother climbed up on to the wall and picked off the enemies one by one with his pistol. As their numbers dwindled, the remaining men tried to hide in nooks and crannies or under beds. At this point a warrior was sent inside with a pitchfork to drive them out of their hiding places into the middle of the room where it was easier to put a bullet in them. The battle ended with every man falling, including the big Spaniard who many had feared would be hard to handle even unarmed. Finally, when all were thought to be dead, feeble-minded Martin was discovered in the cowshed; a cooper from Martinus's ship, known for his simple nature, who had been hiding in a manger all night. The man who found him did not have the heart to kill him, so he led him out to the mob. As the poor soul knelt there, mixing up his 'Christus, Christus', and imploring them not to kill him, Ari Magnússon replied that he should be given quarter and taken into custody. But instead of taking him away, the guards led him into the thick of the mob where one of them split open his forehead with a poker while another struck him from behind with a dung shovel, and with the latter blow that caught him on the back of the neck, feeble-minded Martin fell down dead. This blow signalled the end of the battle, with victory to the Ögur band. The warriors were now eager to divide up all the spoils they had been promised, but at this point there was a change of tune and suddenly all valuables that remained in the wreck or were washed up on shore were declared Crown property and no one was permitted to touch them except Sheriff Ari Magnússon. They were welcome to keep the slain men's bloody rags but Martinus's large, heavy treasure chest and other flotsam salvaged from the shore were taken back to Ögur. As before, the naked corpses of the slain were sunk in the sea, though first various indignities were visited on their bodies, since the commander had announced that the warriors could do what they liked with the dead. So their genitals were hacked off, their eyes put out, their throats cut, their ears sliced off and their navels pierced. After this, holes were bored in the necks and hips of the dead and they were lashed together with rope like stockfish on a string, yet still they kept washing ashore, though they were thrown out to sea again and again for it was forbidden to bury or raise a mound over them, on pain of flogging or being stripped of one's worldly goods. Even the place names of the battlefield were changed for the worse, their beauty fading to match the consciences of those who slew the Basques: where previously the valley had been called Unadsdalur, or the Valley of Delight, now it was merely Dalur, or Valley. Sólvellir, the Sunny Plains, are now Hardbalar, the Hard Pastures. Bjartifoss, the Bright Falls, is now Magrifoss, the Lean Falls. The rocky hillside with its flowery ledges, once known as Sunny Slope, is now the Black Crag. And today at Ögur they call the spit Óbótatangi, the Spit of Infamous Deeds, where once it was the Boathouse Spit, for it was there that most of the bodies washed ashore and long drifted back and forth by Master Ari's landing place, a gift for scavengers and a warning to the servants. Alas, such are the visions that drive an old man outside in nothing but his shirt and stockings into the searing cold of the blizzard on this, the blackest of all nights. But it does not help; the visions will not go away.

THE RED POISON NEEDLE: *a dangerous creature of the shore, slender as a piece of straw. It often lurks in wet seaweed, wriggling and writhing, with jagged stings which can pierce the flesh like a needle. It has been known to cause instant death to young people out gathering seaweed.*

I am swimming. Swimming with strong strokes of my arms, lying just below the surface, the moonlight glittering on my shoulders as they rise briefly from the waves. I turn my head from side to side, breathing in over my left shoulder, breathing out over my right. I kick the water with my feet, sending it foaming about my legs, splashing up from my ankles. I am out in the middle of the fjord, the open sea is ahead; on either side sheer snowcapped mountains tower over stony black beaches. Through the roaring of the sea I hear shouts and yells behind me but I must not slow my pace, I have no time to stop and check how fast the men in the boat are gaining on me. The sea is cold, the current strong, one moment carrying me swiftly forward, the next dragging me many strokes back – I have to know whether I have any chance of reaching shore before them. I stop swimming and tread water for a moment: they are in a trusty eight-oared boat, with a man to every oar and five on the look-out for me, two in the stern and three in the bows, all armed with stones except the fine fellow standing by the mast, balancing easily in spite of the waves. It is this man, Ari Magnússon of Ögur, his fist clenched on a stolen harpoon, who is directing the pursuit. The white breast of my shirt gleams as I roll over on my stomach and start swimming again. I hear a triumphant cry from the boat and a moment later stones begin to rain down around me. One of them hits my right shoulder, bouncing off with a dull thud, but I do not feel it, I am too cold for that. There is only one way to go and that is down. I fill my lungs and dive. Abruptly the world is muted, the strident calls of my pursuers replaced by the underwater hum, the sucking of the waves and my own effortful groans. I dive like an auk, flying through the water with great strokes, like a guillemot beating its wings in the clear shallows on a summer's morning. Deeper and deeper, though the winter sea is not bright but a murky grey – deeper, yes, ever deeper – until I have dived so deep that the air seeks to burst from my lungs and the surface is now too far away. But instead of releasing my breath, I squeeze my throat tight and continue to swim down, though every muscle is on fire as if struck by a sledgehammer. Then the depths in front of me begin to pale; slowly but surely a feeble grey light is filtering up through the soupy sea, and the lower I swim, the brighter and livelier become the motes that whirl up through the water until they shoot past my eyes like sparks from an anvil, three thousand dazzling suns that sting my face like a sandstorm. I give up, abandon my dive. Righting myself in the water, I open my mouth wide, clamp my fists on my breast and shriek as the air is squeezed from my lungs: 'Oh Lord, have mercy upon me ...' When the burning salt sea has ballooned out my body, filling me up to the lips, I am overcome by fatigue and begin to sink. I slip down through the watery greyness, as listlessly as a man picking his way through a bank of cloud on his way down a mountain. High above me, the eight turns towards the shore; Ari of Ögur and his war band have given up the chase. Suddenly it is as if a veil has been stripped from my senses. I can see far and wide through the bottle-green depths of the ocean, far out into the Greenland Sea and in along the bottom of the fjord. There, at the foot of the crag in the middle of the bay, right beneath my feet, is the source of the light: a heart the size of a bunting's egg. It is carved from ebony, polished and girt about by thorns made of horn, with a bronze fire blazing at the top of the join where the two halves fit together – for the ebony heart is half open and inside is the source of light: a tiny crucifix, hung with gilded droplets and stamped with a silver cross. This minute object emits rays so powerful that they illuminate the dreary resting place of the man I have come to find: Peter the Pilot, whose earthly remains lie pinned beneath his sea-smoothed tombstone, a slab of basalt that his murderers threw over the cliff on top of him. His stone-grey hair swirls round his gaping crown where he was struck by the axe, his locks dancing with the deep-sea current like the seaweed entwined among his shattered ribs, which clutches with its weedy many-jointed fingers at the treasure on his gnawed-away breast. He will be able to show this sign at the Pearly Gates on Judgement Day while his tormenters stand empty-handed but for the blood of their victims flowing between their fingers. The moment my feet touch the silt of the seabed, the dweller of the deep stirs. He turns his battered head towards me and bids me good day, although it is past midnight:

'*Angetorre*!'

I return his greeting half-heartedly, for my errand here is never a happy one, muttering a low 'Good evening'.

My meetings with Peter the Pilot always begin the same way: he shoots out the tip of his black tongue, runs it rapidly round his lips, and says quickly:

'*Presenta for mi berrua usnia eta berria bura*.'

I answer sternly: 'Neither warm milk nor fresh butter will be of any use to you here.'

He sighs: 'Long must a dead man wait for a bite to eat ...'

At this point the custom is for me to make the sign of the cross over us and say: 'May the wait for a seat at Our Father's table prove short for us,' thus concluding the formalities. Only this time instead of concurring with the pilot's words, I take out the little brown bundle of canvas containing the splinters of the Cross and hold it up for him to see before tying it to the cord beside the shining pendant. Peter watches me in silence, waiting until I have finished my task and am sitting on the rock beside him, before beginning to speak:

'I am grieved that Señora Sigrídur is dead, my friend. I offer you my condolences ...'

I mutter my thanks.

He continues:

'Yet again the blow has fallen on the same trunk, yet again an innocent person has paid with her life for the support that you gave to me and my comrades, yet again you have been made to bleed for your compassion and courage – no doubt you must find it a perverse sort of gratitude and a poor reward for your good deeds to watch that man of blood growing fat in his high office while your loved ones, great and small, are gathered to the earth ... Long ago you told me that Señora Sigrídur had praised you for refusing to answer Master Ari Magnússon's call to arms against us defenceless shipwrecked sailors, and later for writing a true account of the cruel attack by your neighbours who followed the Sheriff of Ögur – saying that by this action you had kept alive the fine upstanding Jónas Pálmason who had captivated her in her youth.'

'Certainly she was more impressed by this than by my famous deed of laying the Snjáfjöll ghost. Why, she called me the Devil's muck-raker when I exorcised the evil spirit that Reverend Jón had, by his own heartless behaviour, raised up against himself ...'

'She was a good and just woman ...'

'And unsparing in her sense of justice. No doubt I deserved it.'

'You showed courage by turning your back on the very men who had praised and flattered you most for the exorcism; you heeded the call of justice when you bore witness to the atrocities that the perpetrators were confident men would forget ... And by putting your account on paper, you not only recorded the events as they truly occurred, but gave us withered corpses back our vocal cords that the war-frenzied peasants had torn from our throats with their blunt implements ... You sided with the slain against their killers, you stood up to the evil ... As we will testify on the Day of Judgement when the honourable couple, Señor Jónas and Señora Sigrídur, will be rewarded in full for their charity ... Pardon ...'

A crab crawls out of Peter the Pilot's mouth. He coughs and is about to speak again when another, larger crab crawls out. Peter spits up sand. When the third and largest crab begins to force its way out between his lips, it is clear that my meeting with the pilot is over. I kick against the seabed, shoot up from my dive and surface by the cliffs, where I heave myself out on to the rocks. The grey seawater spurts in spasms from my nose and stomach. I start awake: I am lying head down in bed by the hearth, vomiting up my half-digested supper. It is still the longest night of the year.

IV

(Spring Equinox, 1639)

The island rises ... It emerges from the deep as the flood tide strips the waters from its shores ... Fish flee the dry land, out to the dark depths ... Shore birds, newly arrived, follow the ebbing tide, scurrying along the water's edge, pecking around their feet ... The tide-mark retreats rapidly, like a silk glove drawn off a maiden's hand ... A bank of liver-coloured seaweed glitters in the morning sun, swollen and vulnerable ... Ever more is revealed of the neck of black bedrock on which the island sits ... Seaweed flows down over its shoulders ... All around me the world is turning green ... Sap is flowing through the plants, swelling their veins ... Grass that was dull and muted yesterday now ripples on the island's head like brilliant green fire ... The balmy breeze carries the promise of dandelions yellow as suns ... Meanwhile the sea is sucked ever further from the island, swept from the shallows ... The sparse white hairs lift themselves on my skull, blowing down over my brow and into my eyes ... The breeze is freshening ... It is blowing from the east, and just a touch to the south, into Trévík Cove ... Conditions will soon be perfect for what is to come ... I crawl forward to the edge of the Gold Mound and look over ... Today I am hoping to see the island sing, to hear the sound of its form – to confirm that it is a string, pitched in harmony with its Maker ... And why should it not be? Everything here was ordered according to the same rules as everything else that came into being in those six days; yes, even here one is in a harmonious place ... It is easy to think this way when the wind sounds so gentle that it is hard to know whether the whisperings one hears are snatches of its conversation with the grass or addressed to oneself as it wafts past the ear with a soft, soothing murmur ... For it cannot tell the difference between human beings and tiny flowers, as becomes apparent when it blows up a storm ... Now, would it be better to stand here or there? At the highest or lowest point? Up on the Gold Mound or down by Gullbjörn's Cave? Where the island draws breath or where it exhales? But what is that plaintive bleating? I cannot be doing with that ... Where is it coming from? Baaaa ... I leap up and peer around ... A sheep is trapped on its back down by the Elf Knolls ... A stranded black sheep ... Baaaa ... The symphony is about to begin ... It must not be ruined by the bleating of a stranded sheep ... I run down off the mound, if you can call it running, and ramble through the tussocky dells, if you can call it rambling ... I reach the knolls somehow ... The sheep is thrashing around on its back, kicking wildly in the air, and glares at me with malignant yellow eyes before trying to strike at me with its cloven hooves ... I approach the animal from the side and roll it back on to its legs again ... It was its own fault that it got into this mess ... What was it doing grazing in a place like this? The sheep lowers its head, grunting angrily as if I were somehow responsible for its plight ... There is nothing as wrathful as the glare of a sheep that believes it has a grudge against one; no animal seems to believe as unconditionally as the sheep that we govern the world and that every mishap that befalls it should be laid at our door ... The sheep snorts ... I snort back ... Abandoning the idea of butting me, it bounds away towards the shed ... Never mind the music of a whole island, I must make amends for the animal's behaviour ... I clasp my hands over my stomach:

Hidden the house, the mound is green,
wherein the hayfield's treasures sleep.

Well may you prosper, race unseen,
now as ever, rewards to reap.

Hear me, gentle yet potent queen,
elfin lady, dwelling in the deep,
be forgiving now, as you've always been,
to an old man and a foolish sheep.

I hear a voice recite from the mound:

Welcome, well-spoken one,
sage and civil-tongued,
thanks to thee
and thine I will give,
a reward in return
when need requires.

I bow down before her ... Then return to my investigation ... I scan the land from the Gold Mound to the cave: in a direct line between them are two rocks, the middle rock and the southernmost rock, then the Elf Knolls where I stand, and the pond, like the stops or keys on a divinely crafted instrument ... Below them lies the tunnel through the island, a shaft bored from east to west ... Now there will be a great sucking and gurgling as the sea empties from the mouth of the tunnel under the mound, which is covered with water every day of the year except today ... The pipe is clear .... A herring gull flies in from the sea on gleaming wing, riding over the island on the easterly breeze; first over the Gold Mound, then over the middle rock, then the southernmost rock, now the Elf Knolls ... It is right over my head ... I follow its course, spinning on my own axis, catch it reflected in the pond, see how all of a sudden it swoops to the mouth of the cave ... What can the bird want there? Ah, yes, there it gains an updraft under both wings, which lifts it in an arc high into the sky where it hovers, its white-feathered breast towards me, brilliant in the morning sun like a dove over the high altar ... And now another puff comes from the same lung that elevated the herring gull to the clouds ... Invisible lips of air are placed against the Gold Mound ... They blow into the pipe ... I hold my breath ... The blast of air passes through the rock to burst out of the cave mouth on the shore, sounding the first note of the symphony ... It is a low note ... As if the island were joining in with the song ... The ground vibrates beneath my feet ... Small birds fly up ... The sheep take fright ... A newly wakened spider curls into a ball ... Seals slide into the sea ...

The note reverberates long and loud … I close my eyes and my soul begins to vibrate along with it … And I feel a sensation of mingled awe and joy … Then it falls silent as suddenly as it began, the wind drops … I grow cold, my body is covered with gooseflesh, even the taut skin of my leathery scalp … The black sheep stands quite still in the pen, every muscle tensed … He chews uneasily, glaring accusingly at me, as if I have played this noisy trick on him … No, my lad, that bookish old fellow Jónas Pálmason has not the power – though some may think he can twist great forces round his little finger with ease … Look, sheep! Here is one who has amused himself by becoming the plaything of the air: the gull has allowed the noise to carry it still further, still higher, to where its silhouette now circles … The grass begins to whisper again … I start to run; my legs may be decrepit and bent but they will do for a short sprint, such as from here down to the shore … Once there I walk slowly out on to the sand, picking my way prudently over the slippery rocks, taking care not to tread on the slimy seaweed, and station myself where I can see into the cave, bracing myself … Here the sound must surely be loudest … The odour of seaweed carries from the darkness inside, the lapping of pools on the cave floor ... Water drops with a hollow sound on the rocks, the weed .... And in some places the plinks have a brighter tone, as if they are falling on something more precious than wet stone ... There, the old people say, Gold-Björn's treasure is supposed to lie hidden ... Directly below the Gold Mound itself is the gold that gave him his nickname ... A chest full of bright metal ... Fire of the sea god Aegir, tears of Freyja, mouth-fee of the Giant Thjazi, and more gold ... For a long time I wanted to go in search of it, but no more ... I have been deprived of life's luxuries for so long that gold no longer seems desirable to me unless I can make it myself ... But here I have no means to do so ... It seems to me that the roof furthest inside the cave is blue with light ... There the tunnel dips, running down towards the sea, so it must simply be daylight ... The smell of the sea plants grows suddenly stronger ... The breeze becomes a gust ... It sounds as if black-headed gulls are shrieking in the cave ... It is the birds which swarm out by the Gold Mound at the other end of the pipe ... I call in reply: 'Come, wind, come ...' My voice echoes ... The gulls fall silent ... And the gale replies ... A mighty roar hits me, heavy as a waterfall ... It fills my senses, bellowing in my ears, parching my eyes with salt, whining in my nose, bellying out my gaping mouth ... I stagger but manage to stay upright ... I bend and sway like a blade of grass so that it cannot knock me off my feet ... It snatches and tears at my clothes, stretching them over my body ... Breeches and coat-tails whine and crack ... Then it drops slightly ... A little more ... A little lower .... And lower still ... Then hops abruptly up to the fourth rung again ... Sketching a ladder of notes ... Leaping up and down the scale ... Sometimes it blows gently and calmly ... Stopping perhaps for a long pause on a single rung with one airy foot poised, as the other runs wildly up and down the scale ... All at once it has three feet, five ... It howls and shrieks, murmurs and plains, laments and whistles ... There are animal sounds and human speech, whole choirs sing in chorus, whole herds call their names ... What a symphony ... It is as if the east wind is bringing me all the songs of the Earth at once, bellowing out the saddest dirge together with the most joyous paean ... As if he had swept up the news on his journey around the globe, as he passed over continents, wildernesses, forests, nations, farmlands, villages; as he leapt through palaces and houses, under tables and benches, in and out of dark corners, up skirts and down collars ... Before sweeping all he has learnt high into the sky – just beneath the ethereal sphere, where the ravens go to gather news of events that have not yet occurred ... There he kneaded all the news together into thick bales of cloud which he floated like post bags across the sky, sending them hither and thither, adding to them until they were so swollen with story and incident that they were ready to burst, and then he had to find them a way back into the world again ... He rakes together the clouds in the sky, gathering them like a haystack in an embrace so vast that the wind can only just peep over his right shoulder ... He heaves the cloud-stack to and fro, keeping a look-out for a suitable place to set it down ... Then an islet rises in the north at low tide, with a hole through its middle ... The wind opens his jaws wide, stuffs the clouds in his mouth, packing them into his cheeks, knits his brow, stoops down to the islet and lays his mouth to the eastern side ... His name is Euros ... And he blows ... And plays ... And blows ...

—

SOUL FLY: *large and long in appearance, almost in the shape of a man, with red thighs and two legs which hang low in flight, like the redshank when it drives an interloper from the nesting grounds. It has a distinctive singing voice.*

—

I lie in the grass by the pond, quite spent ... The island has fallen silent, the tide is coming in ... I think: how wonderful Sigrídur would have found it to see and hear this ... But fortunately she is on land with Reverend Pálmi, otherwise she would be dead again ... And I think: how newsworthy this would seem to my esteemed rector, the famous, divinely blessed philosopher and defender of bodily as well as spiritual knowledge, the kind-hearted Ole Worm, who took pity on his downtrodden, ill-used little brother in the study of natural phenomena, Jónas Pálmason of Iceland ... How I wish I could send him this musical island in gratitude for having sheltered me awhile under his academic gown; make one of the English herring boats out here on the bay tow the island south to Copenhagen ... But it cannot be done ... I will have to draw it instead ... I will try to send him a drawing ... I am exhausted ... My grizzled head lolls to one side, my arms lie flung out, my legs splayed ... As floppy, I suppose, as a rag doll thrown aside by a child after a vigorous game ... The child has run off somewhere, the doll sprawls in a corner ... So it is when the forces of nature enjoy a fleeting game with one, which ends in an instantaneous victory for the mighty, leaving behind the poor toy with all the unrealised games playing out before its mind's eye; not that anything would ever have come of them ... But today it is neither the gnawing doubt that anything will ever return to its place nor the painful certainty that the mountain will never lack for snow ... It was neither an earthquake nor an avalanche ... Like the game that lingers on in the doll, the music continued inside me ... I am inspired, puffed up with the stories, the poems that the boisterous east wind has taught me ... I feel as if I know all there is to know! The compartments of my body have been filled with all the knowledge a solitary man can possess, alone and unaided by books, schoolmasters, picture stories, wise old dames ... I myself am like a compendium, which inside one thick leather cover contains all the wisdom of the world on many closely written folios, lavishly illuminated and bound up with horsehair string to prevent it from spewing out pages ... Whatever I am asked, about great matters or small, I will know the answer ... I can describe with equal certainty the hoarse mating call of the goosander, the cruel nature of the red-combed whale, the last days of the Greenland colony, polygamy among the Negroes, the explosive force of gunpowder, a certain cure for the squitters, the mildness of the wild pansy ... Nothing, nothing at all, is strange to me any more ... I am omniscient ... A fit of yawning assails me ... I let my mouth gape wide, stroking my face with flat palms ... Breathe in and out with great sucking sounds, quite unafraid that any spirit of the air will sneak inside me ... I clap my hands together: let them come! There is no room any more in this wisdom-stuffed Jónas ... I feel as if at least three spirits are trying to force their way into my mouth at once, seeking an entrance to my body down my windpipe ... I let them rage ... Feel them crashing into my uvula again and again, but they will have to go away disappointed ... My gorge is stuffed like a Danish sausage, full perhaps of lore about the natural history of bean plants and garlic, and nothing that has the merest hint of the selfish character of fallen devils can get past that stuffing; no, only the self-sacrificing breath of life can pass down there, clear, blue and pure, which keeps the heart cool and nourishes the brain ... I sit up ... Rock uncontrollably forwards and from side to side ... Lie down again ... The world may have entered my carcass but that is not to say that it has arranged itself there according to any rational order ... Indeed, how could it? There was too much going on when the symphony rose to its height and the tempo of the notes merged with my own tempo ... For the most part I received it with open arms but there were times when I turned my back or knelt ... Five times the storm of notes knocked me out cold ... I squealed and wailed, bellowed and moaned ... Yes, it entered me in every conceivable manner ... Fire, air, earth, water ... From these elements everything is made, including me ... Whatever was thrust inside me is made of the same substance as myself ... It may be hot, dry, cold or damp ... And so I can find the proper place for everything, as if I were a tall building of twelve floors, very spacious and furnished with cabinets containing many shelves and chests with many drawers ... In the two compartments of my heart I organise everything that is warm, light and spring-like ... Tales of the endearing nature of infants, the deeds of virtuous girls, the unlooked-for helpfulness of wild beasts; healing herbs that must be picked in the morning dew; fair golden jewels made in honour of the heavenly family and other holy beings or else to encase the bones and skin of saints, and of course the pelican ... Some things I launch into my blood, home to all that is hot and damp: many things connected to the world of woman, her work, her womb and her love for her children and husband, though some of her fair things find a place in my kidneys, according to the alchemical order, and some even lower, in the lap, and there I am guided by the rules of astrology ... And so it goes on, as if I were a curator in the great building that houses my collection ... Yes, it is large but dilapidated; the copper shingles on the tower that have not been blown off have turned green, the internal timbers are rotten and the cellar needs mucking out ... I walk from room to room, a large bunch of keys at my belt .... In my mind I go up and down the passageways, open the door to the kidneys, close the door to the bladder, take things out of coffers, hang them from the ceiling, lay them on the examination table ... And so, slowly but surely, I move everything inside me from place to place until it ends up on the right shelf ... One item goes into the brain, another into the liver, others into the limbs ... And when I have placed in the spleen all that is cold and melancholy in the world, governed by the bitter black gall that it cooks in its cauldrons or its natural equivalent in the brew of tribulations – there is far too much of me in there, alas: a container of poison from plants, venomous shells and stones; an etching of the man who murdered his wife by shoving her head in a pan of boiling barley porridge; various sad poems about the dark times we live in, including several by the one who is holding the reins here, such as: 'a coal-black sun of sins now climbs / the skies to light the ways / the defender of such heinous crimes / 'tis obligatory to praise'; the swim bladder of a pike; the blunt blade of the axe used by the eighty-year-old executioner Jón Jónsson to chop the head off Björn 'ladies' man' Thorláksson, taking three dozen blows to sunder the joints of his neck; as well as gloomy clouds and all that sort of black gall rubbish – when all this has been placed in the spleen, an equilibrium is finally reached ... Now at last I can stand up ... I scramble to my feet ... I stand upright ... If an eagle-sighted man standing on the mainland placed a good spy-glass to his eye and scanned the island from end to end, he would get a tremendous shock ... On the bank of the pond at the western end of the island what should he see but a sixty-five-year-old gaffer in a threadbare canvas coat, grey-haired as a head of cotton grass in autumn ... No, if the onlooker's miraculous sight was sufficiently powerful and penetrated deep, he would see not the figure of a man but the building that I feel myself to be ... Built from the trunks of trees that drank water and sprouted from the earth; walled about with bricks of clay hardened in the fire, dried in the air:

A lighthouse at the edge of the world ...

Here I stand, swaying on my feet, imagining myself almost grand ...

CORAL: *coral is the name of a stone which, when it comes to the surface, loosened from the seabed by the tides or fierce storms, is as green as a tree or growing shoot, but afterwards hardens to stone, turning red or variegated according to the colours of the sea floor. It allays storms and bad weather, and is effective against trolls and thunder: wise men say that if it is carried on the person, lightning will not harm the bearer, nor the ship, house or field in which it is found. Nor will the person who carries it be harmed by black magic, for it counteracts sorcery and all wicked spirits avoid it. Some say that* *those who own it will prosper and always be well liked. If it is scattered in a vineyard or in other such places there will be a prolific harvest. Worn about the neck it wards off all ailments of the stomach. And it has been well proved that if coral is heated until it glows, then quenched in warm milk, and afterwards drunk by the man who has no appetite or a gripe in the guts, he will be cured. Some claim that coral must be what the ancients referred to as the work of mermen or dwarfs.*

—

After midday it began to pour with rain, thanks and glory be to the merciful Lord ... There is hope that this terrible winter is coming to an end ... Well, perhaps ... If I am not mistaken, the deathly cold fleet of icebergs still looms outside the bay to the north ... But in this as in other things the good Lord will weigh up the deeds of His children and allot us our condition and fortune according to which side is more crowded when He closes the gates of the soul-pens ... One cannot be certain of an early spring – and yet ... At the summer court gathering last year that kindly, noble man Brynjólfur Sveinsson was elected Bishop of Skálholt, so now he is to be addressed as My Lord

Bishop, along with all the other fine titles descriptive of his wonderful benevolence and charity ... As a result, some of the electors have moved from the Creditum pen over to the better, which is known as Debitum ... The sheep fled the downpour, huddling together in the shed, all except the black sheep which galloped around in the cloudburst until his fleece had soaked up so much of the rainwater that he staggered home, haunches dragging, to join the rest ... There will be a fine stench of wool when he starts steaming ... I leave them to it; my sheep look after themselves, so to speak ... I feed them in the yard in the depths of winter, let them out in spring, spread the remaining tufts of hay in the fields, leave the doors of the shed open ... Of course this is no sort of husbandry, but then I am no farmer, I have no time for that ... I myself seek shelter in my human shed ... I blow on the fire, add a fistful of driftwood kindling, put the small clay pot on the flames and boil the last of the vetch in a splash of milk ... At times I wish I knew the art of smoking tobacco leaves, which seems to me a pleasant pastime for those who have the means ... When I was in the Blue Tower there was a Dutchman who used to smoke tobacco after dinner every evening and would willingly instruct his fellow prisoners in the art ... Before long they were communing alone with their pipes, eagerly drinking in the smoke, saying little, wrapped up in their thoughts ... I could not afford to join the Dutchman's school; ah yes, there are many things I have had to miss out on ... I stir the vetch milk together with a little porridge left over in my bowl from this morning and sit down on the bed ... The mouse now pays me a visit ... She seeks out the warmth, hoping for a crumb, courtesy of Jónas's bad table manners ... She is welcome, I owe her a debt of gratitude ... The little mouse sailed here on the wreckage of a house after the big storm in November ... Where she came from I do not know, but it was clear that a farmhouse had been blown out to sea, and the mouse had guided the flotsam here ... Tatters of the former inhabitants' clothing were sadly tangled with the broken timbers: knee stockings, a coat, undergarments, swaddling bands, but no body parts ... The mouse herself was riding on a battered bed post, quite decently carved, on which one could make out inscribed in plain lettering:

'... NSDOTTIR  THE LORD'S ...'

I perceived immediately that this was an example of the riddle known as Anagramme, which can be used to predict the future, although I have still come no closer to solving it than: 'STRID NOT', 'NID STORT' ... Neither of which satisfies me ... The enigmatic board now hangs over the door inside my hut, while other bits of the flotsam came in useful for firewood or draught-proofing the walls and roof ... This saved my life when the weather was at its coldest in February ... I take a spoonful of vetch porridge from my bowl and shake it out on the floor in front of the fire ... The mouse is there in a flash. Squatting on her haunches like a toddler, she sets about devouring the porridge, raising it to her mouth in her front paws ... Afterwards, she must fastidiously clean her snout, for the porridge sticks to her whiskers as it does to mine ... I burst out laughing, because we are both ridiculous ... She flinches, pauses in her toilette and waits, listening ... I laugh again, a forced laugh this time ... Now the mouse knows that it was only old Jónas and carries on with her ablutions ... My hand lifts of its own accord and gently pats the blanket beside me, reminding us that Sigrídur is not here ... When we used to sit together on the bed, when the wind was blowing a gale, for example, or the snow had drifted over the hut, there were times when this same hand would steal under my wife's shift ... There it would flatten out and slide its palm up the small of her back in a slow caress, proceeding from there up between the shoulder blades to the neck bone, and rubbing the knotted muscles ... Sigga used to enjoy this after a day's toil, for she was always harder working than I and never begrudged me the fact ... In her absence I miss being able to fondle her like that ... 'You have such hot hands,' she used to say when my hand was on its travels, looking at me from her gentle, stone-grey seal's eyes ... Then my hand would want to move lower, down from the shoulder blades, rubbing the poor flesh beside the armpits where the weariness could be sorest ... From there it would slide down her spine, pressing the tips of its long fingers here and there into the muscles that lie beside it ... After this my hand would rest on her hip, where it would lie still for a long while ... Back and palm would draw warmth from one another .... With that my hand's proper business was finished, but there were times when, before slipping back out, it would pause at the sacrum where the spine disappears between the buttocks ... A soft place on a woman ... At that point I always grew thoughtful, and always thought the same thing: this could just as well be the place for a tail, whether furry, feathery or scaly ... And before I knew it I would be investigating and probing the spot ... Mistress Sigrídur used to react quickly, shooting out a hand behind her to grab mine tightly and pull it from under her shift ... She would kiss me on the back of the hand and palm and say: 'Thank you, my dear, that's quite enough ...' For my touch was no longer aimed at pleasing my wife, instead it had turned into a medical probing, in support of the thoughts that had begun to rage in my head: in Tartary there grows a plant called Boramez, the fruit of which is a lamb ... Each plant bears a single lamb on a tall stalk that grows up from the middle of the bush, like a rhubarb flower from a rhubarb patch ... The lamb foetus grows inside the bud, as white and furry as fulled wool, until it reaches maturity and wakens to life with a piercing bleating ... Then the farmers of Tartary harvest their sheep ... They go up on to the moors, their scythe blades flashing, and snip the lambs from their stalks, to which they are attached by the navel like the umbilical cord on human babes ... It must be a noisy job but well rewarded, for the meat of the Boramez lamb tastes like fish, its blood like honey ... This form of generation is similar to that of the little bird called the sea-speckle here in Iceland, which is said to be born from leaves of seaweed, though we do not harvest it ... It is also well known that in Finnmark it rains rodents of the species known as *Mus norvegicus*, which the Finns call lemmings, that do not breed like most other species of furry animals but quicken to life from seeds in storm clouds ... I myself have laid eyes on and handled the dried skin of this creature in the Museum Wormianum ... The tirelessly searching, ever resourceful curator had managed by sheer force of will to have a specimen sent to him from Bergen in Norway, though it is hard to find even in its native haunts, for it suffocates in the meadows at midsummer when the grass grows over its head and its corpse quickly rots away ... In England they reap the benefit of barnacles that give birth to geese, which they were allowed to eat during Lent in papist times because the Church classed them as fish ... It is also widely written that the Egyptians endure plagues of mice, born from the clays of the River Nile, which attack their cornfields and eat up every grain ... Thus we have examples of damp air, plants of land and sea, and river silt engendering living creatures with warm blood ... Not to mention the extraordinary origins of several creatures with cold blood, or else little or no blood at all: sponges grow from the stony sea floor, pearls from shellfish, flies from amber ... As I was reflecting on this, inspired by the feel of my wife's sacrum, it seemed to me that the great strides that natural history has taken over the past few decades have left us confronted with the notion that it is doubtful the Creator placed unbreachable barriers between the species that he scattered around the Earth in the beginning ... Now it seems to us natural philosophers that not only is a connection possible between living beings through various portals in their diversely composed bodies – once I saw a hawkweed growing and thriving in a man's ear – but the Lord has placed in the haversack of every single creature a book containing recipes for all the rest ... From a philosophic standpoint every single species of animal, vegetable or mineral is capable of engendering the rest, and although more often than not physical constraints render such a thing absurd – size difference and the like – the same versatile sap of life flows through them all as that which flows deep down in the earth, taking on the petrified forms of shells, leaves and feathers ... Indeed, if you stroke your finger over the fur of a honey bee and a rat, the feeling is the same, they are sisters in that both are short-haired ... But this merely tells me that rodent and bee come from the same workshop, bear the same hallmark ... More remarkable by far is the rarest expression of this nature, which most closely affects mankind and is abhorrent to all God-fearing people – but which the naturalist must, with God's permission and the strength that He grants him in his mercy, confront, examine, research and investigate – and that is the fact that human women can give birth to cats or indeed lay monstrous eggs ...

—

SIREN FISH: *sings so sweetly that sailors are overpowered by her song if they hear it; the Norwegians are accustomed to sing, chant verse and row like madmen if they hear her calls.*

—

There is a stone called *hysterolithos*, which can be seen in royal collections or illustrated in printed books, that possesses the remarkable nature of being shaped like the penis and scrotum of a man with, above them, a fully formed female vagina ...

What the supremely good and vigilant Lord means by allowing nature to scoop up a morsel like this from His cooking pot is not hard to guess: by demonstrating how easily He can mould the likeness of a man from earthly clay He wishes to warn the frail children of men that He can smash the existing form and cast it anew ... They must take heed of their conduct, cultivate good habits, love one another, fear and worship Him ... And He chooses these particular bodily organs so that the populace will respect the excellent task He has set them: to go forth and multiply and people the Earth ... Which can only be done by reproduction, whereby the man introduces his member into the female genitalia, leaving behind his seed so that it may mingle with her blood, a shoot like a seed in damp soil ... The genitals of woman are the doorway through which the infant must pass, by the process we refer to as labour or birth pangs or birth throes, which terms are witness to the difficulty of the task ... Midwives place healing herbs or stones on this doorway to ease the birth, for the suffering of the daughters of Eve is terrible enough even if we do not deny them the aids that are to be had ... People also speak of a woman's secret door ... But that is a paltry name, expressive of our helplessness when faced with the conundrum of foretelling what lies within and what will emerge from that mysterious hole ... Seldom does a man sit willingly before that doorway, waiting for it to open for the babe that grew from his seed ... Waiting around by a woman's groin and tearing the child from within is rightly women's work ... Yet I myself have been there ... It was during our first flight from the Vulture of Ögur's henchmen ... We had no horse, Pálmi Gudmundur was just nine, Hákon four, and Sigga was carrying our third child ... Winter had begun and our progress was slow ... The human wolves had not yet stolen the chest containing our clothes, books, stones, salts and the other useful objects I had amassed ... Sigga was in the lead, Pálmi Gudmundur followed in his mother's footsteps, and I brought up the rear with the little boy in my arms and the chest tied on to my back ... Evening fell ... The wind picked up from the north ... It became difficult to find one's footing on the slippery grass of the shingle bank, though this was preferable to toiling through the heavy sand of the beach ... When I had to turn my shoulder to the wind to avoid being knocked over, I called to my wife:

'Hold on to the boy, he could be blown away ...'

She paused in her tracks and sighed heavily before answering:

'No, you can do that yourself, Jónas; I'm going to give birth to our child ...'

After which she slid down a gully in the bank to the beach, found a cleft in the lava wall and vanished inside ... Pálmi Gudmundur started to run after her but I told him to come back and look after his brother ... I found the boys shelter from the storm, set down little Hákon on a tussock, tipped the chest off my back and opened it ... While I was gathering together the things that might come in useful for the birth, I explained to Pálmi Gudmundur that their mother was about to undergo a long and terrible torment, that the illness now beginning was one of the toughest and most dangerous a woman could endure and she was not certain to survive, but that it was with the knowledge and will of Almighty God that she should suffer so dreadfully, for by this she was paying off an ancient debt incurred by Eve ... I instructed him to lead his little brother in prayer; together they should pray to the good Lord to protect and bless that honest and God-fearing woman, their mother Sigrídur, and their unborn and unbaptised sibling who was still a foetus in her womb but at this moment wished to be born so that it could fear Him and do good deeds to glorify His Name ... I said that their mother's torments would be so great that they would hear her scream and wail, beg for help and plead for mercy, her lamentations would be shrill and unceasing, she would howl like a wounded beast, so the brothers must pray fervently, raising their thin, boyish voices as loud as they could ... I closed the chest ... Before descending the bank to see how my wife was doing, I made our sons sit on the chest, and there they perched, those two little fledglings of the Lord, Pálmi Gudmundur and Hákon, with their thin shoulders and heads bowed over their clasped hands, piping to God to have mercy, shedding tears and singing psalms to save their labouring mother ... She, meanwhile, was lying propped against the wall at the back of the cave, having braced herself against the rock with her heels in the wet shingle ... Fronds of seaweed fell in a tangle from every outcrop, tiny dog whelks studded the roof like stars in heaven, fragments of mussel shell lay strewn all over the floor, with the odd starfish among them; it was well sheltered from the wind ... Sigrídur had pulled up her skirts; she was silent but sweating profusely ... Eventually, when I had spread out the sheet underneath her and was about to lay the birthstone on her groin, she opened: the child came to the door ... It was the little girl, Berglind, who leapt from her mother's womb like a spring from a rock ... Once the afterbirth had come out and the child's umbilical cord had been cut and tied, I fetched the little lads from their seat on the chest lid and showed them their sister ... They found it an extraordinary notion that such a tiny minnow could endanger the life of a full-grown woman like their mother ... We waited there in the lee of the lava until the wind had dropped and mother and child had recovered their strength, by which time it was morning ... The fervent and effective hour of prayer on the shingle bank had made such a deep impression on Pálmi Gudmundur that he was called to his holy vocation, the ministry ... But how it touched Hákon we were never to know, because before it could become apparent we lost him and his little brother Klemens during our desperate travels in the winter of 1621 ... It still pierces my heart to think how few days of our lives Sigrídur and I were allowed to share with our little boys ... Yet I am grateful and happy that the glorious Heavenly Father should have taken pity on them and pressed them to His nourishing breast when their earthly father was denied all succour and everywhere turned away from the homes of his countrymen with pitiless curses and hissing ... It was no mystery what lay behind those closed doors: they housed cold hearts, as tightly locked as the fist of an executioner about the handle of a whip ... When Sigrídur rose from her sandy-pillowed bed, I noticed that during the birth reddish-coloured pebbles had mingled with the sand under her hips ... I gathered several handfuls of them, which I put in our chest, and they turned out to be brother of haematite ... Right up until the day that we were robbed of the chest, Sigga would use these healing stones to ease the birth pangs of many a woman ... For just as the human foetus dwells and grows in its mother's secret womb, unknowable and as likely to take on the form of a beautiful girl as the most misshapen wretch, so nature breeds in its lap both unimaginable horrors and precious gems ... And the anterooms of their birth chambers are the clefts and fissures in the body of the Earth, caves like the one in which my little Berglind was born ... I lean back in bed, stretching my arms and cracking my joints ... The mouse is still huddled cosily by the fire; it is quite extraordinary how she puts up with my ramblings ... The vetch porridge has hardened in the bowl; I scrape out the leftovers and scatter them on the floor ... In a place of entertainment like this it is the storyteller who must pay his audience rather than the other way round ... Mousey nibbles at the food, pricking up her ears at my voice ...

CONCH SHELLS: *several species of conch are found in Iceland. Wise men make use of our edible conches by burning them until they glow, then quenching them in ox urine and giving the fish to the patient to consume in food or drink without his or her knowledge; it protects the maid against man's lechery and the lascivious against intemperate fornication. Also, those afflicted with seasickness may go secretly to the beach and swallow the raw fish out of the shell three times during the waxing and then the waning moon, with a sip of sea-water each time. If people eat a lot of them, they will become too drunk to stand; a condition that we call 'conch totters', which can be slept off. The conch mostly crawls up out of the deeps from the middle of Pisces onwards.*

A rock cavity can also be called a cave ... Shallow caves are often known as grottos, from the Latin word *grotto*, which also means 'small cave', and *grotto* is the stem of the word used in southern countries to describe a particular kind of decorative picture or *grotesque* ... I saw many such pictures in Ole Worm's library ... They appeared in the frontispiece of large tomes of learning, in the margins, in chapter openings or between sections ... For the modern master printers think like the scribes of our old Icelandic manuscripts, who wove sphinxes and chimaeras into their illuminated capitals and the decorated borders of their books ... A centaur here, an old woman with bird's feet there, a three-headed dog ... Bibliophiles as they were, the scribes understood better than anyone that little curios like these provide longed-for staging posts for the readers' eyes on their monotonous descent down the ladder of the pages, word by word, from left to right, along one line and down to the next ... And offer the mind respite from the matter ... If one watches a river of lava, or clouds of steam or great torrents, or a field rippling in the wind, the eye and mind will not rest until they have tracked down familiar images in the flow ... Even though these figures are never still, never clearly defined, never whole, never the same, one's mind can grasp them merely by blinking ... Then time ceases to flow like a river and becomes instead a series of moments which may follow fast upon one another's heels yet each has its own unique form ... The grotesques are just like those fleeting images that I myself have often perceived in smoke, lichen or clouds ... It is as if the artist has transferred the image from the surface of his eye to the page without stopping to wonder whether it is believable or scientifically accurate ... Pictures the draughtsman saw with his eyes and thought up in his imagination have become in an instant part of our visible world ... Oh, those pictures! ... Oh, those thousands of freaks and interwoven absurdities that invigorated me when I was stumbling my way through the thick volumes in the Museum Wormianum ... One never knew where one creature began or ended ... A goat's hind legs might, on closer inspection, turn out to be the beginning of a flower stalk ... But the stalk sprouted not petals but stork feathers, on top of which sat a cluster of butterfly wings ... Nor was it certain whether the goat's body was made of flesh, mineral or vegetable ... And even if one was fairly sure that the lower half of its body was made of marble, it was just as certain that blood flowed through its stony veins ... Was the blood red and hot or green and cold? Everything grows from something else, as if nature were forever having second thoughts, pausing, pursuing a new idea or changing its mind halfway: a blue bird's wing extends from a small boy's temple, but by the time one reaches the tip of the wing the feathers have changed into bright green cabbage leaves with foam bubbling over the edges ... A cat sits not on hindlegs but on a tail, which swells from the hip and curls up under its breast in countless joints like a lobster tail, while the cat's nose is formed from a bunch of berries and about its neck is a collar studded with precious gems ... And one asks oneself: if the pet is this odd, what on earth can the owner be like? A crown of flies' wings rests on the head of a woman with nine udders dangling from her chest and stomach; she has no arms and her legs are like two scaly serpent bodies twined together ... The old Icelandic scholar Snorri Sturluson would not have approved ... For as he says in his *Skálda*, or Handbook of Poetry:

'It is a metaphor to call the sword a serpent and name it rightly, so that the sheath is its path and the baldric and fittings its skin. That is to stay true to the nature of the serpent, for it slides out of its skin and also to water. Here the metaphor is so contrived that the serpent goes in search of the river of blood when it slides down the path of thought, that is, into the breasts of men. A metaphor is thought to be well conceived if the notion that has been adopted is maintained throughout the verse. But if a sword is called a serpent, and later a fish or a wand, or changed another way, people call it monstrous and regard it as spoiling the verse.'

Balderdash, I say, let the sword turn into an adder and the adder a salmon and the salmon a birch twig and the birch twig a sword and the sword a tongue ... Let it all run together so swiftly that it cannot be separated again ... The twilight portents have toppled the world from its foundations ... It is slipping out of joint ... It has been turned upside down ... The heavens are used to walk upon ... While the common populace crouch on their upturned roof beams, hanging from their fingertips, or fall off weeping, the libertine armies rebel against the Creator, using sorcery to turn themselves upside down in the air, dancing their loathsome war dance on the roofs of His celestial abode ... The din of the portents reverberates through the gloom ... God's houses are trampled and kicked to pieces by stamping, bounding, newly rich magnates and their trinket-greedy wives ... Squealing like a sow in season, grunting like the boar when he clambers on her back, they hammer their iron-heeled shoes and lethal spurs on the cloudless, night-blue, star-studded outer walls of Heaven as if they were the beaten-earth floors of brothels strewn with sawdust, or the grey floorboards in the smoke-filled back-rooms of the merchants' halls ... The laughter of the dancers mingles with the starving cries of their humblest brothers and sisters ... Yes, old Snorri's teachings are a thing of the past, even reason is at a loss when it comes to describing the libertine world ... While the colony on Greenland still endured, useful wares made by the Eskimos were brought to Iceland, the most important among them being protective clothing made of sealskin and polar-bear pelts – the Eskimo women must have been skilful with their needles ... Yet among them were objects that no Christian should possess, such as the pagan caricatures called *tupilaks* ... Grandpa Hákon had an ugly little demon like that, carved from wood and decorated with small bones and a patch of human skin with the hairs still attached ... He kept quiet about this possession, hiding it under the floorboards in his study ... The creature had the body of a dog, flayed from its snout to the tip of its tail, protruding ribs and vertebrae like the teeth of a saw, but instead of a dog's head it had the skull of a child, which faced over its shoulder as if its neck had been wrung and it had frozen back to front; its belly, on the other hand, was the face of an imp, grimacing with enormous teeth and eyes on stalks, while between its hind legs the beak of a whimbrel took the place of a prick and beneath its tail a seal's head could be glimpsed, forcing its way out of its arse ... The story went that this bizarre object had been carved for the purposes of witchcraft ... It was said that the sorcerer had with his magic gifts seen the demon inside a piece of driftwood and whittled off its bonds, and as a reward he was permitted to send it through the air to assail his enemies ... Oh, there would be no question what was happening if one met a familiar like this ... Indeed, I think one would resort to defending oneself by sending it home again ... The story goes that the one who originally raised it should point at the *tupilak*, saying angrily: 'It was I who freed you from the wood' ... At which the demon will be disempowered, for of course it knows its own foolish form ... And the sorcerer is saved for now ... Though he will not be so fortunate on the Day of Judgement ... But not all evil spirits are as misshapen as this, not all are as easily recognisable ...

LAVER: *laver grows on rocks by the sea, and is known by some as Mary's weed or slake. It is often baked between hot stones to make cakes like cheese. Eaten in hot milk, laver gives a good night's sleep. It can also be dried like dulse.*

If my daughter Berglind had been allowed to live, I would have asked her to find me one ... And if Sigrídur and I had been as fortunate in our home as we deserved, I would have told the girl to meet me in the smithy ... There I would have told her to look in the woodpile for a piece of wood for us to carve ... Whereupon she would have asked me:

'What should it be like, Papa?'

And I would have answered:

'The knottier the branch, the more twisted and misshapen, the more bent people call it, the harder it is to find it a place among the smooth planks, the more people agree that it should be thrown on the fire, the more useless it is, the more unsuitable for anything except letting one's imagination run riot, the more I covet it, the more I yearn to weigh it in my hand, the more I long to let my whittling knife be guided by its knots and veins ... Yes, bring that piece to me ...'

And while we, father and daughter, each whittled away at our crooked branch, I would have spoken to her like this:

'If a virgin meets a stray horse on a moorland path she sees only a horse. It stands there on the moors, whole and undivided. Yet her youthful eyes have already jumped from one end of the beast to the other, and her mind has added up the body parts, checking that everything is in place: legs, head, body, hooves, tail, mane and muzzle. "There's a horse," the virgin's mind says to itself with such lightning speed that the girl does not even hear it. She thinks no more of it and continues on her way, unconcerned. Yet it is often a near thing, for the girl must not only keep in mind the horse's legs, head, body, hooves, tail, mane and muzzle; it is not enough that every part is in its place; she must also pay heed to which way round the parts turn. For if the horse's hooves face backwards, it is a *nykur*, a kelpie or water-horse, and will want to kidnap the girl, lure her on to its back and gallop away with her to its dwelling place deep in the cold moorland tarn ... Remember what I say, Berglind: if you meet a horse in the countryside, look at its hooves. If the horse is standing knee-deep in grass, hiding its feet, walk steadfastly away. If there is a pond gleaming behind the figure of the horse, you must take to your heels. And should the *nykur* lure you on to its back with the intention of carrying you down into its wet lair, you are to shout its secret name: "Nennir". And it will throw you off. For in common with the other instruments of darkness it cannot bear to hear its name, unlike good spirits which grow and gain strength if one names them aloud and sings their praises. Remember my words, Berglind' ... That is how I would have talked to her, administering a fatherly warning ... For the *nykur* is like man in that it is hard to tell the bad from the good ... Though man has one advantage ... If you meet a man on a moorland path it does not matter whether he is standing in deep grass or on hard-packed snow ... Hmm, I wonder which part of Ari of Ögur faces backwards? My thoughts drove me out of the hut ... I wandered along like a sleep-walker and came to my senses here at the tip of the rocky bank which forms the island's northern harbour ... Baaa ... One more step and I would have walked off the end ... Fallen into the sea, sunk like a stone, drowned ... But the black sheep bleated loudly and woke me from my reverie ... Now we are quits ... Baaa ... When I looked at the sky I saw the grotesques in the evening clouds spreading and stretching beyond the limits of reason and understanding ... They are like bladderwrack spread out to dry on the rocks ... And as the eye travels from one strange beast to the next in search of the boundaries between them, it moves from one joint to another ... Wanders among countless joints ... There is no beginning or end except in the whole undivided picture, in all its parts ... One can never say for certain which limb or body belongs to which entity, for the branches and shoots are all equally valid ... The thought has crossed my mind that it is the joints themselves, the places where the parts meet that are the eternal and absolute in this world, for they exist and at the same time do not exist except as the gaps that connect the most unrelated phenomena ... And the gaps between the limbs that the joint connects can be incredibly small, as small as the gaps between the tiny legs and feet of a bluebottle ... Or they can be vast, the distance so immense that the human eye cannot comprehend it, cannot see the poles even though one is standing midway between them, or is aware of only one limb and knows nothing of the other ... It is in these invisible halls that I believe God dwells ... As was proved long ago when the Roman general Placidus rode out on the stag hunt in the forest by Tivoli ... When the hunter drew back his bow, intending to fell his quarry which at first sight appeared to be what he called to himself 'a fleet-footed stag' – but the dawn sun rephrased, calling it 'a dew-bedecked deer calf, lord of all beasts, his antlers glowing against the sky' – he had a vision of the glorious Christ ... Yet the divinity does not luxuriate in a labyrinth of blazing gold antlers, or pride himself on the light-bordered tines: no, he exists in the cool morning air between the branches of the beast's intricate crown ... It seemed to General Placidus that he saw the boy Jesus standing on the young stag's forehead, resting on one toe and holding out his arms to bid him, a pagan, welcome into his Father's kingdom ... Love flew into his breast ... The quarry felled the hunter ... Placidus took the name Eustace and entered into the service of love ... And was scorned ... Robbed of all his goods ... Tortured ... Forced to flee ... His sons were devoured by wolves and lions ... His wife was ravished by pirates ... Yet he continued to sing the praises of goodness ... He regained his wealth ... Had more children ... Refused to take part in the Emperor Hadrian's burnt offerings ... Was imprisoned ... And with his wife and young children was put on a grid and roasted alive in his persecutors' oven, burnt to ash in the bowels of the idol, a giant bronze ox ... The martyr became Saint Eustace ... Good to call on in times of terror if one's family is in peril ... The antlers of a hart, coral, spread fingers, birch twigs, a loosely knotted fishing net, crystals, river deltas, ivy, mackerel clouds, women's hair ... diverse as these phenomena are and formed from opposing elements, nevertheless they all revolve around the invisible joints, their opposite forms touch even though they are far apart ... and if I imitate their form, reaching my arms to the sky – moving them together and apart in turn, waving them to and fro – then Jónas Pálmason the Learned is no longer alone ... I am the brother of all that divides, all that curls, all that intertwines, all that waves ... after the day's rain showers the web of the world becomes visible ... the moment night falls, the beads of moisture glitter on its silver strings ... nature is whole in its harmony ... twit-tweet ... as can clearly be seen if one treads a dance here on the harbour bar ... twit-tweet ... but it all gets into a tangle if one tries to classify it according to reason ... the strings refresh the eyes and mind ... it is difficult to grasp them ... twit-tweet ... welcome back from the sea, brother sandpiper ... twit-tweet ... it is high tide on the island of Patmos ... the strings run through me ... twit-tweet ... I thrum them ... alas, now I miss my picture books ... twit-tweet ... geyser-birds ...

The Tail or Leftovers

And so we leave Jónas Pálmason the Learned in that happy hour, a frail old man dancing with the universe. We will not join in with his cries of joy when his exile on Gullbjörn's Island is revoked without warning in the summer of 1639. We will not follow him to Hjaltastadur, where Reverend Pálmi Gudmundur will give him a roof over his head for the fifteen years that remain to him. We will not sit with him at his writing desk when he is finally at liberty to tap from the barrel of his brain all the learning that he has accumulated during his long life, which he now sets down on paper for his patron, Bishop Brynjólfur Sveinsson: his biographical poem 'Sandpiper', his writings on natural history, his little book of herbs, his commentary on the Edda, the legends, outlaw ballads, genealogies and pictures of whales – and the many other texts that made this book possible. We will not be present when a seventy-year-old Jónas secretly has a child with a maid, a boy, named after his father, who inherits half his nickname, becoming Jónas 'the

Little Learned'. We will be absent but we will send our respects when he dies in 1658 and at his own wish is buried crosswise before the church doors.

So we say:

'Farewell, brother Jónas, and thank you for entertaining us. That is sufficient now, we have enough on our plates with our own twilight portents ...'

Jón Gudmundsson the Learned comes to his senses in pitch darkness. His clothes are soaking, yet he is warm to the bone. He is reclining on his back in a fairly shallow hot pool. His arms lie close against his sides, his legs straight out; he is as stiff as a board. The back of his head rests on the soft bed of the pool. The thick, viscous water reaches up to his temple and fills his ears, making all sounds deeper, more remote. Jón half rises, stiffly, waiting for the shiver of cold. It is very hot in this dark place, the air even hotter than the water, as when a large saucepan comes to the boil. The shiver of cold does not materialise. Jón heaves himself out of the warm liquid, stands up, misses his footing on the slippery floor and half falls: the whole place is moving gently, like a ship in a light breeze. He squats down and leans his head from side to side, letting the water run out of his ears which are now assailed by a heavy, rhythmical booming, a tremendous distant roar of water rising and falling, and a sucking noise.

While Jón the Learned was asleep – or swooning – he dreamt that a man came to him in a grey-brown homespun coat, with a grey-speckled cap of the same material. Under the peak of his cap gleamed beady brown eyes, surrounded by feathers. The man leant towards Jón, laying his thick, powerful beak to his ear, and chirped in a low voice:

'When you awaken you will have forgotten your name; for all you know, you may be called Jónas Pálmason.'

Jón finds the dream bizarre for that is his name: Jónas Pálmason – generally known as 'the Learned', but sometimes called a painter, or more rarely an ivory-smith.

Jónas the Learned makes another attempt to stand up and this time he is successful. He rides the wave, picking his way gingerly over the slippery floor. This must surely be a cave, wide and high-ceilinged here where Jónas is standing, narrowing as it deepens, and yet it is constantly on the move.

How on earth did he get here? The last thing Jónas remembers is standing on the end of the curved lip of lava that forms the northern harbour on Gullbjörn's Island. The tide was at its height and he retreated from the wave when it licked the toe of his shoe. Then the surf began to break on a reef out in the harbour where there had been no reef before. Jónas had waited a little, craning his neck to see what was rising out of the water. It was black and the sea foamed over it, for it was moving fast. Before he could even scream with fright, a great fish had swallowed Jónas.

He knows the species; Jónas the Learned knows that he has been consumed by a north whale; an evil leviathan that grows to eighty or ninety ells long and the same in width, and its food is by all accounts darkness and rain, though some say it also feeds on the northern lights. In spite of this knowledge, Jónas reacts to his discovery like a man. Judging by the length of his beard and his hunger pangs, he calculates that he has been lying unconscious in the fish's belly for three nights and two days. It must be going to spew him up on to dry land. Jónas gets on all fours and crawls out of the stomach, up through the gullet, into the head and takes a seat on the animal's tongue.

After swimming all day the north whale comes to a halt. It opens its jaws. Light floods into the fish. It takes Jónas time to grow used to the brightness, but soon he sees that the beast has rested its chin on a grassy bank on the shore, as if its lower jaw were a drawbridge, and at the other end of the bridge he glimpses two human figures, one splendidly robed, the other dressed in black. It is Jónas the Learned's unfailing benefactor, the excellent Bishop Brynjólfur Sveinsson, in full regalia, a mitre on his head and golden crosier in his hand, and his loving son, Reverend Pálmi Gudmundur Jónasson, Minister of Hjaltastadur. Jónas sets off at a run, racing over the slippery tongue as fast as his feeble legs can carry him, out of the whale's mouth. There he throws himself flat on his face, pouring out tears of gratitude, kissing the bishop's feet. Reverend Pálmi Gudmundur kneels down beside his father and raises him up. They fall into one another's arms with a great shedding of tears.

The Bishop of Skálholt smiles blithely at father and son. Raising his gloved hand, he makes the sign of the cross over the leviathan. The great fish slams its jaw shut, gives a splash of its tail and disappears once more into the deep.